"You wanted to see me?" Cassandra asked uneasily

"I asked you here to advise you to spend less time with Hugh," he said. "It was a tremendous blow for him when his wife found someone else. I don't want to see him hurt again."

Cassandra's eyes widened in astonishment. "I'm sure it never entered his head to regard me as anything but a woman out of her element here. He's a *friend*, the only person on board I'm comfortable with," she said hotly. "Just because you..."

A wave of color swept over her face as she remembered how she'd panicked in Nick's arms.

"You can't even handle being kissed by me," Nick said knowingly. "How are you going to cope if he sees you as more than a friend?"

But Cassandra knew it wouldn't happen.

Books by Anne Weale

ANTIGUA KISS
FLORA
SUMMER'S AWAKENING

HARLEQUIN PRESENTS

HARLEQUIN ROMANCE

These books may be available at your local bookseller.

Don't miss any of our special offers. Write to us at the following address for information on our newest releases.

Harlequin Reader Service
P.O. Box 52040, Phoenix, AZ 85072-2040
Canadian address: P.O. Box 2800, Postal Station A,
5170 Yonge St., Willowdale, Ont. M2N 6J3

ANNE WEALE

frangipani

Harlequin Books

TORONTO • NEW YORK • LONDON
AMSTERDAM • PARIS • SYDNEY • HAMBURG
STOCKHOLM • ATHENS • TOKYO • MILAN

Harlequin Presents first edition December 1985
ISBN 0-373-10846-X

Original hardcover edition published in 1985
by Mills & Boon Limited

CHAPTER ONE

'*Aloha!* Welcome to the Pacific.'

Before embracing the girl she had come to meet at Honolulu airport, Rosalind Vernon lifted a *lei* of carnations and tossed it deftly over her younger sister's fair head.

Her own hair was a rich dark chestnut inherited from their mother. She wore it flowing down her back with the stem of a crimson hibiscus flower tucked behind her left ear. A clinging white crochet top outlined the full curves of her breasts and very brief white cotton shorts showed off her high, rounded buttocks and a pair of long golden-brown legs poised on high-heeled red ankle-tie sandals. A small dark red eelskin disco bag dangled from her shoulder, and her toenails and long fingernails were painted to match. She was elaborately made up and, before the arriving passengers had begun to emerge from the Customs hall, had attracted a great many stares from other people waiting to greet them.

Those who saw the person she had been waiting for were surprised when it turned out to be a young woman whose appearance and manner were in marked contrast to Rosalind's.

Cassandra Vernon had been in transit for twenty-four hours. She had been deeply asleep when one of the stewardesses on the penultimate lap of the long flight from Europe had roused her because they were coming in to land at Honolulu. There had been no time to go to the washroom and freshen up, or to change into lighter clothes as had been her intention.

The beautiful garland of flowers which her sister had draped over her shoulders only served to emphasise the pallor of her thin, tired face and the inappropriate heaviness and drabness of her navy blue pleated wool skirt and cheap, travel-crumpled blouse.

She glanced down at the thick rope of petals. Then her long lashes lifted and her weary grey eyes met Rosalind's sparkling blue ones with their curled and mascaraed lashes and fashionably shadowed lids.

'It's beautiful . . . thank you. Oh, Ros, it's so good to be here!'

Her low voice trembled a little as she held out her arms to hug the much loved older sister whom she had seen only once since the terrible row with their father when Rosalind was eighteen and Cassandra four years younger.

In the intervening six years Professor Neville Vernon had never once mentioned Rosalind. He knew that she and Cassandra wrote to each other, but he never asked for news, and Cassandra never dared to volunteer information for fear he might forbid her to continue the correspondence. She had always been afraid of her father, sensing that he blamed her for the loss of his wife who had died when Cassandra was born prematurely.

'It's great to have you,' said Rosalind, when they drew apart. 'I was afraid Father would be an invalid for years and that you would never get away,' she added frankly. 'It must have been awful for you, having to nurse him for so long. I couldn't have stood it. But it's over now. Let's forget it,' she went on hurriedly. 'How was the flight? Not too good, by the look of you. If you'd travelled first class you would have enjoyed it. Flying tourist class is only bearable on short hops.'

'I can't afford to travel first class,' said Cassandra. 'Coming here at all is an extravagance. But I couldn't resist the chance to spend a few weeks with you and meet your fiancé. Has he come with you?' she added, glancing about, half expecting to see her sister's husband-to-be hovering a few feet away, waiting to be introduced.

'No, he's looking forward to meeting you, but today is a big day for him. There's a championship golf tournament being played at Kapalua Bay and Harley is a fanatical golfer,' Rosalind explained. 'He wouldn't miss it for anything. Is that all your luggage?'

She looked at the one small suitcase which the younger girl had put down a few moments earlier.

'I didn't have much to bring. Looking after Father, I haven't needed many clothes and I couldn't buy summer things in England in November. It seemed best to wait until I got here. I've a cotton skirt and blouse in my flight bag. Is there somewhere I could change? Or isn't there time?'

Cassandra knew from her sister's last letter to her that one more short flight remained before she reached her destination, the Hawaiian island of Maui where Harley Dennison's yacht, *Ocean Wanderer*, was berthed.

'There's no hurry. You can change in the restroom. You must be boiling in that thick skirt and pantyhose,' said Rosalind, with a glance at her sister's nylon-clad legs and low-heeled serviceable shoes.

It was only the difference in their footwear which made her seem the taller. Both girls were above average height, but it was their sole resemblance. In every other respect they could scarcely be more dissimilar.

Rosalind walked with the short steps dictated by her four-inch heels and with a provocative swing of her hips. She didn't offer to carry the suitcase and Cassandra didn't expect it. Two years of caring for her partially paralysed father had given her strong arms and shoulders. She could have handled a much heavier case with ease. Taking one pace to three of Rosalind's, she walked alongside her through the bustle of the airport, relieved that the long hours of travelling were almost over.

How long *Ocean Wanderer* would remain at Maui she didn't know yet. Rosalind and her American fiancé were in the process of crossing the Pacific Ocean from Canada to Australia, and Cassandra had been invited to join them for the passage from Hawaii to Fiji.

In the airport restroom she unzipped her nylon flight bag and took out the top and skirt she had intended to land in. The white cotton top had been made in India. She had bought it from a market stall in the centre of Cambridge, the English university town where she and her sister had been born and grown up.

The full skirt of pale grey cotton with a spriggy design in white was one she had had several years. It had come from the Cambridge branch of Laura Ashley, whose inexpensive but stylish clothes were very popular with the female undergraduates and other Cambridge girls.

However, when Rosalind saw the grey skirt her eyebrows shot up. She said, 'How long have you had that, for heaven's sake? It looks long overdue for the ragbag. You can't arrive wearing those things!'

Cassandra was taken aback. 'Can't I? Why not? I thought on a boat the rule would be cool and casual.'

'Casual, yes—not way out of date.' Rosalind glanced at her watch. 'We'll have to dash into town and buy you a couple of things to wear tonight and tomorrow.'

The prospect of a hurried shopping expedition when she was already wilting from the unaccustomed humid heat made Cassandra's spirits sink. She was longing for a bath and a rest.

'If these things really won't do, couldn't I borrow something of yours for the time being?' she suggested.

'My things wouldn't fit you properly,' said Rosalind, looking at their reflections in the mirror behind the washbasins and comparing their figures. 'We may be about the same size, but we're a different shape. Anyway, I never lend my clothes. Come on: change into those for now and we'll take a taxi to the Ala Moana mall. It isn't far.'

A little more than an hour later a taxi returned them to the airport just in time to board the flight to Maui.

'You look a different person,' said Rosalind, with an approving glance at the transformation she had wrought in the short time since her sister's arrival. 'You'll look better when you've worked up a tan, but at least you don't look like Orphan Annie any more.'

Cassandra was not as happy with her changed appearance. She was not keen on any of the clothes which Ros, seconded by an effusive saleswoman, had insisted were perfect for her. But she had been too jet-lagged to resist their combined pressure on her.

She had even been obliged to submit to having some make-up applied by a girl demonstrating eye make-up techniques in the cosmetic section of one of the stores in the large shopping mall they had visited.

This she had tried to resist, but Rosalind had overruled her objections with a forcefulness it had been difficult to combat without seeming rude and ungracious to someone who obviously meant to be kind and helpful.

The aircraft on which they flew to Maui was tiny compared with the giant B-747, seating more than four hundred passengers, on which she had flown from Europe.

'Most people fly in to Maui by the airport at Kahului, which is about twenty minutes from Honolulu,' explained Rosalind. 'We're going to the little airstrip at Kaanapali on the west coast. That's the side with the best hotels and golf courses.'

'Golf and sailing seems an unusual combination of interests,' commented Cassandra.

Although the champions were younger men, she regarded golf as a game for the middle-aged and elderly and had never known a young man who played it. However, considering that she had spent the first twenty years of her life in a city swarming with young men, she had known very few. Rosalind had rebelled against the rules and regulations imposed by a disciplinarian father, whereas Cassandra had acquiesced—not because she was biddable by nature but because, during her teens, she had been more interested in horses than in boys and discos. At seventeen she had begun to take an interest in the opposite sex. But before her eighteenth birthday her father had had a stroke and all her hopes and plans for the future had had to be shelved for the task of looking after Professor Vernon.

'I must say golf bores me to death,' Rosalind confided. 'But I don't mind Harley being crazy about it. His mania for golf leaves me plenty of time for shopping. A lot of American women take their husbands and boyfriends shopping with them, but I can't shop with a man in tow.'

She inspected her shiny red nails. 'Tomorrow I must have a manicure. You could do with one too,' she added, with a critical glance at the younger girl's short unvarnished nails. 'You shouldn't have dishpan hands at your age. You must have been doing housework without wearing rubber gloves.'

'I'm afraid I have,' Cassandra admitted. She noticed that although Rosalind was wearing several rings on her smooth, manicured fingers, the third finger of her left hand was bare. 'Where's your engagement ring?' she asked.

'I don't like to see diamonds at the beach, which is where I spend a lot of my time,' was Rosalind's reply. 'Gold jewellery—in moderation—looks good with a suntan, but I think diamonds look flashy. My ring spends most of its time in the safe Harley has on board. He spent a lot of money on it and I should hate to lose it or have it stolen, which could happen. Even though we're anchored offshore, it wouldn't be impossible for someone to sneak on board and steal things.'

Even if she hadn't been dazed from sleep, Cassandra's seat on the aeroplane from Vancouver had been too far from a porthole for her to see Honolulu from the air before they landed. But her place on the smaller aircraft gave her a good aerial view of the city and the adjoining beach resort of Waikiki with its clusters of highrise hotels. It did not look the kind of place which appealed to her.

As little girls, she and Ros had spent many summer holidays with their father's elder sister, a retired unmarried schoolmistress who lived near a famous wild life sanctuary on the bleak, windswept east coast of England. Cassandra had loved to swim in the chilly waters of the estuary near Aunt Esmée's cottage when the tide was right. She could hardly wait for her first dip in the warm turquoise seas around Maui.

Along the coast where the plane began its descent, the beaches and rocky coves were a mass of rooftops grouped around patches of bright blue which she recognised as swimming pools. As the aircraft swooped lower and lower she could see people stretched out on sunbeds on the decks surrounding the pools.

A few minutes later the aeroplane landed on a runway only a few yards from a wide golden beach with waves breaking on it.

'Now all we have to do is to take a taxi to Lahaina and before you know it you'll have your feet up and a long, ice-cold drink in your hand,' Rosalind promised.

The first part of the road from the airport to the place she had mentioned was lined with a beautiful tall hedge of bougainvillaea in many colours—crimson, magenta, pink, white and coral. On the seaward side of the road were the rolling fairways and smooth greens of a large golf course. Between this and the sea was a line of very large hotels surrounded by extensive grounds where the fronds of tall palm trees fanned gracefully in the breeze.

'That's the Hyatt Regency Maui. It cost eighty million dollars, and there are two million dollars' worth of Oriental works of art in the grounds,' said Rosalind, indicating the last and largest of the group of hotels they were passing.

It was clear she expected her sister to be impressed, and Cassandra tried to look as if she were. But it was the wonderful multi-coloured hedge, which Rosalind had not even glanced at, which impressed her more than the costly buildings. Privately she thought them rather an eyesore.

A few kilometres further on the taxi left the main coast road and entered the outskirts of a town where many of the gardens had beautiful flowering trees and shrubs growing in them.

Presently the residential district gave place to a long waterfront shopping street crowded with tourists, some of whom had overdone their sunbathing and whose shoulders and legs were now an unsightly and painful-looking lobster red.

At the far end of the street, between a timber-built hotel and an enormous banyan tree, the taxi turned down a side street leading to a marina. Here the two girls got out and Rosalind paid the driver.

'There should be a boat waiting for us.' She led the way along the dock, passing several game-fishing cruisers and booths where people could book trips on them.

Cassandra expected their transport to *Ocean Wanderer* to be a rowing boat or possibly a rubber dinghy with an outboard motor. What she had not expected to find awaiting them was a small launch with a uniformed seaman sitting in it, listening to a Sony Walkman. He was only a youth in his late teens, and his uniform consisted of white shorts and a white tee-shirt with *Ocean Wanderer* printed in blue on the chest. But his presence was a surprise, because Rosalind hadn't mentioned that Harley had anyone crewing for him.

As soon as he noticed Rosalind the youth whipped off the headset and prepared to help them aboard.

'This is Olaf,' said Rosalind, as he reached up to take her sister's suitcase.

She didn't complete the introduction, and instead of saying hello the young man gave Cassandra an oddly respectful nod.

'I'll go tell the Captain you're here. He's at the library,' said Olaf, when the sisters were seated in the launch.

His accent was a combination of Scandinavian and American.

'The Captain?' queried Cassandra, as he sprang on to the dock and set off in the direction of the hotel they had passed.

'Nick Carroll . . . Harley's skipper.' Rosalind opened her bag and took out a pack of cigarettes and the gold lighter she had already used several times since Cassandra's arrival. Before lighting up, she added, 'I call him Captain Bligh. Not to his face, of course. Harley says he knows the Pacific like the back of his hand. He's spent his whole life sailing round it. But he's an unsociable type when he isn't forced to be pleasant, and God help the crew if they step an inch out of line. He's even had the cheek to lecture me!'

'What about?'

'He doesn't approve of smoking, especially not at sea. At the start of the voyage I was given a long harangue about not throwing my cigarette ends out of the portholes or over the side in case they were blown inboard and started a fire.'

A non-smoker herself, Cassandra could see the point of the Captain's homily.

'To be fair, a fire at sea is a pretty terrifying

contingency and there are a lot of careless idiots who
might chuck a butt overboard. There've been dozens of
hotels burnt down by people smoking in bed and setting
fire to the bedclothes,' she answered. 'Ros, how big is
Ocean Wanderer? I had no idea she had a professional
skipper and a crew.'

Rosalind drew on her cigarette, inhaling deeply. 'You
didn't imagine I would cross the Pacific on a small
boat, did you?' she asked, raising her eyebrows.

'It depends what you mean by small. I visualised
something like that.' Cassandra pointed to a thirty-foot
ketch which looked as if she would accommodate at
least four people in reasonable comfort.

'Not likely!' was her sister's emphatic comment.
'There ... that's *Ocean Wanderer*.' Rosalind pointed
out the vessel which belonged to her fiancé.

Cassandra gasped. A few minutes earlier, while Ros
was paying the taxi fare, she had taken a quick look
round and noticed an old square-rigged brig moored
close to the balconied façade of the hotel. But the only
other large ship in sight had been what seemed, at a
glance, to be an inter-island cruise ship anchored out in
deep water.

A closer inspection showed that it was actually a
miniature liner of the kind owned by Greek shipping
magnates and American business barons.

'Harley would have to be a millionaire to own that!
You're joking ... aren't you?' she exclaimed.

'Certainly he's a millionaire. How could he afford to
support me if he weren't? I have very expensive tastes
these days,' said Rosalind laughingly.

Her expression changed. She looked into her sister's
startled eyes and said seriously, 'And before the end of
this trip I'll line up a millionaire for you. It won't be
difficult if you play your cards right.'

She meant it, Cassandra realised, aghast.

Before she could protest that she didn't wish to have

a rich husband found for her, a voice from behind them said crisply, 'Good afternoon.'

Turning, they both looked up at the unsmiling dark face of the tall white-clad man standing on the edge of the quay a few feet behind them and well within earshot of Rosalind's last remark.

Their father had been a tall man, but also a thin one with the stooped shoulders and indoor complexion of a dedicated scholar. The man scrutinising Cassandra with an anything but cordial expression in his hard grey eyes looked as if he had spent every day of his life in the sun and much of his time engaged in physical activities. Heredity had given him a large bone structure and either his work or his leisure activities had armoured his big frame with muscle.

At the same time his facial features suggested a keen intelligence as well as physical power. She concluded he must be the Captain's chief mate or first officer, or whatever the second in command on a private cruise ship was called.

When Rosalind said, 'Oh ... hello, Nick,' it gave Cassandra her third shock within a few minutes.

From what her sister had said about *Ocean Wanderer*'s Captain having spent his life in the Pacific, she had visualised him as a man in his fifties or older.

Captain Carroll looked to be in his early thirties, although a lot fitter than many of his contemporaries. There was no suspicion of incipient flab round his lean middle, no thickening of flesh at the sides of his taut, square jaw.

'Cass, this is Nicholas Carroll, our Captain and, when we're at sea, our complete lord and master,' said Rosalind, in a provocative tone to which some men would have responded with an affable disclaimer.

Not Captain Carroll. Acknowledging the introduction with a nod and a clipped 'How d'you do?' he leaned over the edge of the quay to hold a string bag of books within their reach. 'Take this for me, would you, please?'

Although politely phrased, it was an order rather than a request, with a definite suggestion of 'And look sharp about it!'

Rosalind, her sally ignored, reacted by ignoring his somewhat peremptory instruction and saying, 'Will Olaf be long? My sister has had a long trip. She's very tired.'

As Cassandra took hold of the books and sat down with them, he answered, 'Olaf is staying ashore. As soon as you're seated, Miss Vernon, we'll be on our way.'

Pouting, Rosalind sat down. As he joined them in the launch and turned to untie the mooring line, she pulled a childish face at his back, then looked at her sister and shrugged.

The pout and the furtive grimace were a sudden vivid reminder to Cassandra of the unhappy relationship Ros had had with their father. Admittedly Professor Vernon had never been a loving, tolerant parent, but then Rosalind's behaviour during her mid-teens had been calculated to worry and exasperate the most easygoing father. She had never tried to keep on the right side of him, or of anybody in authority over her. She had always been good at alienating people and bad at getting along with them. It seemed that the years hadn't changed her; except, presumably, where Harley Dennison was concerned.

If Rosalind knew that Captain Carroll was a dour, stiff-necked man, it had been foolish of her to make that saucy remark about his absolute authority when the ship was at sea. She should have known it wouldn't amuse him.

On the other hand it was pretty offhand on his part to say only a curt 'How d'you do?' and not to add a word of welcome or any kind of civil pleasantry.

Perhaps his unfriendly manner had something to do with his overhearing Rosalind's promise to find a rich man for her sister. It was unfortunate he'd heard her say that. If already he didn't like her, such a statement could only increase his antipathy and make him inclined to categorise them both as gold-digging opportunists. Which was not true.

Or was it?

Abruptly Cassandra realised that just as her assumption about the size of *Ocean Wanderer* had been wrong, her assumptions about Harley might be equally inaccurate.

I hope not, she thought worriedly.

She had been so relieved to hear that Rosalind's succession of affairs with unsuitable men had finally led to a more stable relationship with one who wanted to marry her.

As she and Harley hadn't known each other long, the voyage across the Pacific would give them time to be absolutely sure of their feelings, Rosalind had written to her sister. If all went well, as she felt certain it would, they would be married in Sydney.

Now the unwelcome possibility that Ros was embroiled in yet another misguided relationship loomed out of what Cassandra had hoped was going to be, literally and metaphorically, a clear blue sky.

As the launch left the small marina and headed for open water, she forced herself to concentrate on admiring the view of Lahaina and the mountains rising behind it. By now it was late afternoon, but the sunlight was still very bright and she realised that what she should have bought in the shopping mall was a pair of sunglasses. She had never needed them in England and, unlike all her school friends, she had not been abroad for holidays. This journey to the Pacific was her first taste of foreign travel and she was determined to wring every ounce of enjoyment and interest from it.

'Lahaina looks quite an old town. What kept it going before tourism?' she asked her sister, raising her voice against the sound of the outboard.

'I've no idea.' Rosalind had her back to the coast and wasn't looking at it over her shoulder. She was trying to prevent her hair from being blown about as the launch gathered speed.

It was Captain Carroll who answered Cassandra's question.

'Lahaina used to be a whaling town. In the eighteen-forties there'd be up to four hundred American whaling ships anchored in this roadstead.'

She turned to look at him. The peak of a white-topped flat hat shaded his forehead and straight dark eyebrows. His short-sleeved white open-necked shirt had blue epaulettes on the shoulders. The visible part of his long legs, between his shorts and the white stockings turned over below his knees, were as brown as his sinewy forearms. His uniform had less gold braid than that of a senior naval officer, but he was the kind of man who didn't need braid to emphasise his air of command. There was something about him which in any clothes and any context would suggest a leader, a man endowed by personality and training with the ability to direct other people's actions.

Cassandra shifted her position to be within easier conversational distance of him. She ventured a smile before she said, 'It must have been a wonderful sight . . . a forest of twelve hundred masts. What is that old sailing ship lying near the small boat harbour?'

'She's *Carthaginian*, a replica of a whaling brig which is used as a small museum.'

His reply, polite though it was, somehow lacked the ring of a real desire to share his knowledge. She sensed that, without exchanging more than a few words with her, he had written her off as a girl of little intelligence, unworthy of more than the basic minimum of attention.

Cassandra wasn't a vain girl. She knew that her looks were average. She wasn't a stunner like Ros. At the same time she wasn't unhappy with her face or her figure, and her sense of self-worth certainly wasn't so low that she could accept being written off by a stranger on the basis of a few minutes' acquaintance.

'Thank you,' she responded stiffly.

She turned away to look towards *Ocean Wanderer* and, deliberately, remained sitting with her back to him until they came alongside the boarding ladder where a Polynesian member of the crew was waiting to help them to step from the launch to the companionway.

When, from force of habit, Cassandra would have picked up her suitcase, Captain Carroll forestalled her.

'Atu will bring your case for you.'

Atu was a tall, beefy man with a thick black moustache and perfect teeth exposed in a broad beam of welcome. It was one of the most radiant smiles she had ever encountered, the more striking in contrast to the Captain's poker face.

Before she put her small pale hand into the large dark brown hand extended to help her, she noticed that Atu was wearing the *Ocean Wanderer* tee-shirt, but in place of shorts he had a straight wraparound skirt of navy drill. His big feet were bare. She didn't think he was a Hawaiian but had no idea which other group of islands he might come from.

She had already seen that the ship had more than one deck. They arrived on board on the lower one from which a wide companionway with polished teak handrails led to the upper deck, a large part of which was covered by a blue awning.

'The crew live somewhere below. Our cabins are on this deck, and we eat and relax on the top deck,' Rosalind explained. 'I'll show you your quarters. This way.'

Cassandra wouldn't have minded had she found that

her accommodation was one of the cabins with portholes just above the waterline. To be ushered into a twin-berthed deck cabin charmingly decorated in a cool and fresh combination of green and white was unexpected luxury.

'Oh, Ros, how pretty ... and how comfortable!' she exclaimed, looking round at the clever use of space which gave plenty of storage for two people's belongings and no sense of being cramped, although the cabin was actually smaller than a bedroom.

'And how tidy you've become,' she added teasingly. 'Your bedroom at home was always in chaos— remember? This is as neat as a pin. Have you reformed, or does someone keep it tidy for you?'

'I have a stewardess, naturally,' said her sister. 'But I'm not sleeping in here. I'm on the starboard side. Here's Atu with your case ... and Mrs Shane to unpack for you.'

Mrs Shane was a small, grey-haired woman in a neat navy overall with *Ocean Wanderer* embroidered in white on the breast pocket.

'Good afternoon, miss. I expect you'll be glad of a shower after your long trip.' Her accent sounded Australian. 'If you'll give me your keys, I'll have everything unpacked and shipshape by the time you've finished in the bathroom. You'll find all you need in there, from a shower cap to a bathrobe.'

'Yes, I'm longing for a shower,' Cassandra agreed. 'But you needn't trouble to unpack for me, Mrs Shane. I haven't brought very much with me.'

She saw Rosalind frowning at her from behind the stewardess's back and gathered she had said the wrong thing.

'It's no trouble, Miss Vernon. That's what I'm here for. But if you'd prefer to unpack yourself, I'll come back later and see if there's anything you want pressed. I'm very handy with an iron, and it doesn't do to leave creases in longer than necessary.'

'Thank you. That's very kind of you.' Cassandra
smiled warmly at her, sensing that from this motherly
little woman she might receive much needed counsel on
the ways of an alien environment.

'It's not kind of her. It's her job,' said Rosalind
shortly, as soon as they were alone. 'You should have
let her unpack for you. Although on second thoughts, if
the rest of your clothes are like the things you arrived in
perhaps it's better for her not to get a close look at your
wardrobe until we've done some more shopping. Mrs
Shane is a talker, and we don't want her telling other
people that you turned up practically in rags.'

'I'm sure she wouldn't dream of saying such a thing.'

'Not as baldly as that, but obliquely she might. I
don't want her hinting to people that we haven't any
money.'

'It would only be the truth. We haven't,' Cassandra
said wryly. 'Father's illness used up all his savings.'

She longed to let go her feelings and to have Ros hug
and comfort her as she had when they were both
children and if Cass had been hurt or frightened she
had turned to her sister for mothering. But that was a
long time ago, and already she sensed that in the years
they had been apart Ros had changed even more than
her letters had suggested.

Their reunion was too recent for either of them to
behave as spontaneously and lovingly as they had once
done. That close affectionate intimacy would revive,
given time. But Cassandra knew that this wasn't the
moment for her to break down in tears and expect Ros
to take it in her stride.

With a great effort she managed to master her
emotions and say huskily, 'But let's talk about all that
later. I can't wait to dive into that shower! See you
later.'

Cassandra woke up. In the first instant of consciousness,

before she opened her eyes, she thought she was still in
an aeroplane, shortly to be served with yet another
plastic tray of airline food. Then her eyelids lifted and
with delight she recognised the luxurious cabin with its
moss-coloured carpet and green and white décor.

How long had she been asleep?

After her shower she had unpacked and then lain
down for a quick cat-nap, expecting to be woken a few
minutes later by Mrs Shane coming back. If the
stewardess had returned she must have decided not to
disturb the new passenger's snooze. The digital clock
which was part of a panel of switches and press buttons
showed that Cassandra had been sleeping for almost an
hour. It was probably time for her to be making herself
presentable for her first encounter with her future
brother-in-law.

She had not yet bestirred herself and was wondering
what time they dined on board and whether the evening
meals were informal or dress-up affairs, when the cabin
door opened and Ros peered round the edge.

'Oh, you're awake now.' She stepped inside, her
appearance resolving the second of her sister's
uncertainties.

Clearly dinner aboard *Ocean Wanderer* was very
dressy indeed. Ros was wearing tight black silk pants
with a loose gauzy black and gold top with huge sleeves.
The neckline was high, but through the diaphanous
fabric her beautiful breasts were visible. She had
repainted her face with a dramatic evening make-up
and she brought into the cabin a delicious, sensuous
gust of expensive French scent.

Cassandra sat up. 'You look marvellous!'

It was true. Her sister did look marvellous. Not in a
way which Professor Vernon or Aunt Esmée, or the
teaching staff at the girls' boarding school where both
her nieces had been educated, would have admired.
Indeed they would all have been horrified by

Rosalind's glittering glamour. It was neither 'well bred' nor 'in good taste'—their two highest terms of approval. It was flamboyant and sexy and, worst of all, 'out of place' on board a yacht, even one of this order.

Nevertheless Cassandra had to admire the panache with which her sister wore the outfit and the perfect figure which enabled her to carry off the clinging pants and see-through top.

'Thank you.' Rosalind paused to admire her reflection in the mirror behind the dressing counter. Then she came and perched by Cassandra's feet.

'Listen, Harley has brought back some people he met at the tournament today. They're American and very animated and I think, being tired from your trip, you'd find them rather a strain. I suggest you have supper right here on a tray in your cabin and then catch up some more sleep. You can meet Harley tomorrow when he's stopped rabbiting on about this bloody boring tournament.'

'But won't he think that rather rude of me?'

'Not at all. He already knows that you've been through one hell of a time with Father and I'll tell him you're wiped out by jet-lag. If you don't appear for two days, he'll understand. There's plenty of time for the two of you to get to know each other. Now, what would you like for your supper? We've two chefs on board, and they can whip up whatever you fancy.'

'I'm not really very hungry. An omelette and perhaps a bit of salad?' Cassandra suggested.

'Right: I'll go and order it for you. By the way, if you find yourself awake in the small hours you can make yourself a cup of tea.' Rosalind opened a locker containing an electric kettle and other equipment. 'Or fix yourself a drink.' Another door revealed a small refrigerator stocked with canned drinks and bottles. 'And as you can see, there are plenty of books and magazines to read.'

Half an hour later, when Mrs Shane brought her supper tray, Cassandra asked her how long she had been on *Ocean Wanderer*.

'I came back to sea three years ago, after my husband died. At that time the owners were Sir John and Lady Carstairs,' the stewardess told her. 'He was one of the wealthiest men in Australia, but his family had had money for generations and he was a perfect gentleman. Not like some who have money nowadays,' she added, pursing her lips.

'You spoke of coming back to sea. Had you been at sea before you were married?'

The stewardess nodded. 'You could say the sea's in my blood. My father was Engineer with old Captain Carroll—the present Captain's father. Mother never liked the sea. You can't blame her. What woman wants to be left on her own most of the time? She was always warning me never to marry a mariner. My first job as a children's nurse was with a family at Rose Bay, which is one of the posh parts of Sydney. I was with them for ten years, looking after three babies. Then Captain Carroll's wife had her baby and it did something to the nerves in her spine, so she couldn't walk. But she was determined to go on living on board her husband's ship, as she always had, and the Captain asked me if I would consider becoming their nanny.'

By this time she had finished transferring the things on the tray to the writing table. As well as something under a silver cover—presumably the omelette—there was also a covered soup cup from which Mrs Shane removed the lid before drawing out the chair and waiting for Cassandra to seat herself.

'None of my brothers wanted to follow in Dad's footsteps,' Mrs Shane continued. 'But I'd always had a hankering for the seafaring life. So I looked after Captain Nick from the age of six weeks until it was time for him to go to school. What a to-do that was! He didn't want to be packed off to Australia and he tried to get out of it by . . .' She paused. 'But that's a long story and your soup will get cold if I tell it. Enjoy your supper, Miss Vernon. I'll come back later to clear away.'

The soup, cream of chicken, not out of a tin, was excellent, as was the rest of the light meal. As she ate, Cassandra wondered if she had been mistaken in sensing that Mrs Shane did not rate the present owner of the yacht as highly as his predecessors.

She had also had an intuitive feeling that Rosalind's suggestion that she should eat in her cabin had not been motivated solely by consideration for her sister.

Maybe it wasn't the Americans being a bore for me which Ros was afraid of; but of me being a bore for the Americans, she thought, as she finished her supper with pineapple mousse served in a long-stemmed glass goblet, with a crunchy topping of chopped nuts with a flavour she didn't recognise.

'They were macadamia nuts,' Mrs Shane enlightened her, when she returned. 'You'll have to ask Captain Nick about them. He'll know. He knows most of the answers to the things passengers ask. You'll meet him at breakfast tomorrow, unless you sleep late. He's an early riser, like his father.'

'I've already met the Captain. He brought us over in the launch.'

'And what did you think of him?' Mrs Shane enquired, very much in the tone of a fond parent inviting praise of her favourite son.

The truthful answer was: I thought, for the Captain of a cruise ship, he was amazingly dour and disagreeable.

But she couldn't say that to a woman who had been a second mother to him.

'He's very much younger than I'd expected,' she answered. 'I thought he'd be at least middle-aged.'

'He'll be thirty-five in February. That is young to be in his position. He's been at sea all his life, except for the few years when he had to go to school.'

'You were going to tell me what he did to try to avoid that,' Cassandra reminded her.

'Yes, but it'll keep for another time. I should let you catch up your beauty sleep. It's a long, long way from England to Maui and you must be exhausted.'

Perhaps regretting that her ready tongue had led her to the edge of an indiscretion, Mrs Shane finished loading her tray and bade Cassandra good night.

When she had gone, Cassandra went into the adjoining bathroom to brush her teeth. Lingering traces of eye-liner on her lids reminded her that earlier, before having a shower, she had been dismayed to discover that the make-up put on by the demonstrator had done nothing to enhance her looks. Applied to her tired, pale face it had served to make her look rather tarty and hard.

Perhaps, what with the make-up and the sexy red dress, plus what he had overheard Ros saying as he came up behind them, it wasn't surprising that Captain Carroll had formed an unfavourable impression of her.

Presently, lying in bed with the lights out, she thought about her sister's fiancé now entertaining his guests on the deck above. Would he like her? Would she like him? Was Rosalind sharing a cabin with him?

The thought made her move uneasily. When she had imagined they were crossing the Pacific on a sailing boat, she had taken for granted that even though turns on watch might make it difficult for them to sleep together in the literal sense, they would be lovers. How could an engaged couple alone on board a small boat on the world's largest ocean not be on terms of the closest intimacy?

But that was a different matter from sharing a cabin on a yacht as large as *Ocean Wanderer* where the nature of their relationship was not a private matter but would be known to everyone, including the Captain.

For the first time it occurred to her to wonder if Captain Carroll had a wife. Not many heterosexual men were unmarried at thirty-four. But if he had a wife, surely she would live on board with him as his mother had lived with his father? Mrs Shane would have mentioned her.

She yawned and turned on her side, enjoying the comfort of the firm mattress and the soft down pillow and the feel of the fine percale sheets. It was bliss to be able to stretch out and to know that tomorrow morning, and every day thereafter until she had to go back to England, the sun would be shining.

The cabin was still in darkness when she woke. The fluorescent numbers of the digital clock showed 2:17. As Rosalind had forecast, Cassandra's body-clock had told her it was time to get up and here she was, wide awake, in the middle of the night.

Having made herself a pot of tea, she drank two cups and looked through a magazine. What she wanted, she realised, was some exercise.

Next to walking, her favourite exercise was swimming. Suddenly it struck her that, as long as she was very quiet, she could have a swim now. It was a bright moonlight night. The sea was calm. Provided the boarding ladder was still in place she could slip into the water without making a noise which would disturb people sleeping on that side of the yacht.

A few minutes later, wearing the black one-piece which had been the regulation bathing suit at her boarding school and with a bath towel over her arm, she left the cabin and crept along the central passageway which led to the deck where she had come aboard.

The ladder was still there, the platform at its foot suspended a couple of feet above the shining surface of the sea. Leaving her towel on deck, Cassandra made

her way down the ladder. On reaching the platform she
sat down and dangled her legs in the water, which felt
wonderfully warm and silky.

After sitting there for a few minutes, looking towards
Lahaina where a few lights showed that she wasn't the
only person awake, she lowered herself into the sea and
began to swim slowly away from the yacht's hull. Seen
from this perspective, the vessel looked huge, her decks
far above Cassandra. The round portholes close to the
water-line were presumably those of the crew's quarters.

About fifty yards of breast stroke followed by the
same distance of back stroke toned up all her muscles
and made her feel back to normal after the long hours
of being airborne or confined to airport lounges.

She was lying on her back, floating and studying the
stars, when a sudden strong swirl in the water made her
gasp with fear.

'Oh, God, you gave me a scare!' she exclaimed, when
she recognised Captain Carroll treading water beside her.

'Get back on board immediately,' he said, his voice
quiet but furious.

Cassandra didn't argue. Her heart still pumping
wildly from the fright he had given her, she made for
the boarding ladder.

It was only when she had felt the movement in the
water that she had suddenly realised that at this
latitude, in deep water, there might be sharks. Even
now, with him swimming behind her, the possibility
that their movements might have caught the cruel little
eye of a cruising predator sent a sharp thrust of terror
through her.

Fighting down panic, she forgot about being quiet
and swam as fast as she could for the safety of the
ladder. Normally she could have hauled herself on to it
with ease. But tonight her arms felt like jelly and she
couldn't heave herself out. As her first attempt failed
and she slumped back into the water, the man beside

her pulled himself on to the platform in one fluid movement. Then he reached down and grabbed hold of her. An instant later she was on the platform beside him.

'Bloody stupid girl!' he snapped harshly. 'Don't you have any sense? People don't go swimming alone at night in the Pacific. Even inside the reef it can be dangerous.'

As she stood there, trembling and speechless, he pushed her roughly aside and went up the steps to the deck, two at a time. It was only after he had disappeared from view that she realised he had been naked.

Cassandra waited until her heart had stopped pounding. She took some deep calming breaths. Then, still shivering, as if the balmy night had turned cold, she climbed the ladder.

She had thought that by now he would have gone back to his quarters and any further reprimand would be delivered tomorrow. It was disconcerting to find him near the top of the ladder, drying himself on her towel.

'Oh . . . I'm sorry,' she muttered, instinctively turning away from the unfamiliar sight of a nude male.

But as she started to hurry away, he said curtly, 'Wait.'

Cassandra halted, but she didn't turn round. She had neglected to squeeze the water out of her hair and it was streaming down her back.

'You can have your towel now.'

When she didn't react immediately, he added, 'I'm decent.'

She turned. The towel was spread over the varnished wood rail at the top of the white-painted guard rails. Captain Carroll was in the act of fastening a piece of coloured cloth which covered him from waist to knee.

'You'd better come up to the bridge. We can't talk here. Get dry first,' he ordered.

What Cassandra would have liked to do was to wrap the towel round her dripping head, tell him their talk would have to be postponed until tomorrow, and walk away to her cabin. But the upsetting events of the last few minutes had shattered her normal self-possession. Intimidated both by the man and his manner, she did as she was told.

On top of everything else, it was a humiliating experience to have to rough-dry her hair and have a cursory rub down while the wretched man stood there watching her, his arms folded across his bare chest.

By moonlight he looked almost as dark-skinned as the Polynesian steward. The light bronzed the powerful muscles which had scooped her out of the sea. His face was largely in shadow. But after one rebellious glance she did not look at him again until, moderately dry, she wrapped the towel round her body to cover the unflattering black swimsuit.

'This way.' He turned on his heel and led the way up to the top deck.

As she followed him she combed her hair with her fingers, trying to tidy the tousled mop resulting from her hasty towelling.

A brief survey of the upper deck showed that it had three main areas. Towards the stern it was open to the sky. Then came the section covered by the awning. This was furnished like a luxurious terrace with comfortable chairs and chaises-longues and white-lacquered woven cane tables.

Amidships the deck was enclosed with walkways on either side. As they passed along the starboard side, going in the direction of the bows, she glimpsed through the windows on her left a dining-room with one long table, clothed but otherwise unlaid, surrounded by about ten chairs.

A little further along he went up a short flight of steps leading to an even higher level. There he opened a door and switched on a light. A moment later she was inside the bridge, overlooking the bows of the vessel and another triangular deck with half a dozen sun-beds arranged round a splash pool.

'Sit down, Miss Vernon.' He indicated a swivel seat on a metal stem bolted to the deck.

When Cassandra sat in it she realised that it was the Captain's seat, adjusted to suit his long legs. Her own legs weren't short, but her feet couldn't rest on the deck. They dangled like a child's, making her feel even more at a disadvantage.

She decided her only hope of retaining any dignity was to admit she had been foolish and to apologise.

Before she could open her mouth, he said, with a snap, 'Most of the accidents which happen to visitors to these islands are caused by their own stupidity. You're not a child, Miss Vernon. You should think before you act. From now on, for your own safety, don't swim except in daylight and never on your own. The danger from sharks or barracuda isn't high if swimmers use some common sense. But only a few days ago a local fisherman trapped several sharks close inshore. You're lucky I saw you out there. Even if nothing worse had happened to you, you'd have found yourself trapped in the water and having to shout for someone to come and pull you out, and that would have woken the whole ship. You should have made sure you could get out before you went in.'

'I'm sorry I put you in the position of having to risk your own safety,' she answered stiffly. 'But if what I was doing was so dangerous, I'm surprised you didn't stay on board and whistle to attract my attention. Waking up a few people would seem a more sensible act than risking *your* neck for me, Captain.'

His lips compressed in a hard line. Anger flashed in the cold steel-grey eyes. Clearly he wasn't accustomed to being answered back.

Edging herself off the chair, she stood up and, with frigid politeness, said, 'Will you excuse me? My wet bathing suit isn't comfortable. I'd like to go and change.'

As she would have walked past him, he stopped her by stepping in front of her.

'One last piece of advice, Miss Vernon. You're going to be on this ship for a number of weeks. You'll enjoy the trip more if you don't put anyone's back up—particularly mine. If you're asked to do something, do it. If you're warned not to do something—don't. And please try to act considerately towards the stewards and the stewardess. Mrs Shane is single-handed at present. She'll be kept very busy when the rest of Mr Dennison's guests fly in. You can help her by keeping your cabin in reasonable order and not expecting her to press your dresses at short notice.'

'I don't know why you should think me deficient in basic good manners, Captain Carroll,' she said hotly. 'It seems to me that is *your* failing. You've been noticeably antagonistic since the moment we met.'

The tall Australian didn't reply for a moment. He seemed to be making a decision.

Finally he said, 'There are more laudable ways for a girl to get on in the world than by looking for a rich protector, Miss Vernon. For instance, by working for a living as most of your sex do.'

It was obvious he was referring to Rosalind's statement at the small boat harbour yesterday afternoon.

Cassandra said, 'My sister was joking, Captain Carroll. I'm amazed you took that remark seriously. I'm not looking for a rich husband, and I'm sure my sister is marrying Mr Dennison for his personal qualities, not his money.'

He said drily, 'You haven't met Mr Dennison yet, have you?'

'What do you mean by that?'

He gave a slight shrug. 'It was merely a statement of fact. Go and get changed, Miss Vernon. You don't want to get a chill on your first day aboard.'

He stood aside to let her pass.

CHAPTER TWO

WHEN she woke up for the second time, bright sun was flooding through the ports and the digital clock showed 11:03.

Tidying the cabin, after she had showered and dressed, reminded her of Captain Carroll's unwarranted injunction to her not to make unnecessary work for Mrs Shane. The recollection made her frown. Then, catching sight in the mirror of her annoyed expression, she made up her mind not to allow that man or anyone else to take the edge off her pleasure in this once-in-a-lifetime trip to romantic places.

All her life she had longed to travel, and now here she was, on the far side of the world, and nothing and no one was going to mar her enjoyment.

In this determinedly buoyant frame of mind she sun-creamed her face, arms and legs and, in the tee-shirt and shorts she had worn last summer for gardening, went on deck in search of Rosalind and the man she was engaged to.

The first person she met was Atu, who gave her his big happy smile.

'Good morning, Atu. Do you know where I'll find my sister?'

'She's gone ashore, miss. She left a message for you that she would be back for lunch.'

Clearly he spoke English fluently.

'Is Mr Dennison on board?'

'He's playing golf, miss. Can I bring you some breakfast?'

'I don't think so, thank you. I'll wait until lunch.'

'You should have something to eat. We usually serve

coffee or tea at eleven. Some fruit won't spoil your lunch.'

Cassandra agreed to have some, and presently Atu came up to the sun-deck with half of a fruit she had never seen before. It looked like a giant pear with a thick golden-green skin and pale orange flesh. The centre had been hollowed out and filled with yoghurt, and some slices of what she recognised as a lime were arranged at the edge of the dish.

'It looks delicious. What is it?' she asked, as the steward placed it at her elbow.

'It has two names—papaya and pawpaw. Lime juice improves the taste,' he explained, starting to pour out coffee for her.

She tried a spoonful. The juicy flesh combined the flavours of peach and melon. It was as delicious as it looked.

'Mm . . . very good,' she murmured. And then, as he seemed disposed to linger, 'Which part of the Pacific are you from, Atu?'

'I come from Fiji,' he said proudly. He waved in the direction of Maui. 'These islands are okay, but not as good as Fiji.'

'Have you been on this ship a long time?'

'As long as the Captain . . . four years. My father was greaser for his father, but now I am Chief Steward,' he told her, in the same tone of pride with which he had spoken of his homeland.

'What kind of ship were you on before this one?' she asked.

'We have been on many kinds of ships, even a big cruise liner such as *Royal Viking Star* which carries seven hundred passengers. When the Captain leaves, I shall go with him. We have always been together . . . like brothers. But he is clever and I'm not,' he added, with a laugh.

'Is the Captain leaving *Ocean Wanderer*?'

'No, but maybe some time. One day he will have his own ship. Not like this. With sails.'

At this point another man appeared. He was wearing an officer's uniform but was not much older than Cassandra, with a blunt-featured pleasant face and alert hazel eyes.

'Good morning, Miss Vernon. I'm Chris Knight . . . Fourth Officer. When you've finished your elevenses, would you like me to take you along the coast for your first swim? There's a nice bathing beach not too far from here.'

'That's very kind of you. I'd love it. Can you give me fifteen minutes?'

'Half an hour if you like. There's no hurry as long as we're back in time for lunch. Have you got a beach wrap with you? You shouldn't have your shoulders uncovered for more than about fifteen minutes the first day.'

'I know, and I'm not going to risk getting burnt. All my exposed parts are smothered with sun-cream,' she told him.

'Good, because it's really strong and you've plenty of time to work up a nice tan slowly. People with two weeks' vacation are inclined to rush it—usually with painful results. See you in about twenty minutes.'

Atu had already gone. While she finished eating the papaya, Cassandra wondered if the Fourth Officer had offered to take her swimming off his own bat or had been ordered to do so. As he had been in uniform, the latter seemed the more likely. Would her emergence from her cabin have reached the bridge, or wherever the Captain spent his time when the yacht was at anchor, as quickly as that? Perhaps after speaking to her, Atu had served the Captain's mid-morning coffee and mentioned that she was up and about.

The apparently close relationship between the two

men seemed unusual and interesting. She could understand them being friends as children. The interests and pleasures of small boys were much the same the world over. But differences of race and education tended to become more divisive as people grew up. It wouldn't have been surprising if they had found themselves having less and less in common as the years passed. Perhaps the fraternal feeling between them had survived because they were both men of the sea to whom the motion of the ship, whether violent or almost imperceptible, was more natural than the feeling of the land under their feet.

Her beach wrap was actually a white voile dress shirt of her father's, with fine hand-stitched pin-tucks down the front. She was wearing it over her swimsuit when the Fourth Officer handed her into a large rubber dinghy with an outboard.

By the time they arrived at the beach they were on first name terms. Chris was a Canadian who had joined Harley Dennison's yacht after starting his career on tankers.

'But that's a pretty dull life. In fact being at sea at all plays hell with a guy's social life,' he told her when, after some energetic swimming, they were both bouncing up and down amid gentle breakers. 'I was lucky to get this job through some friends who knew Captain Carroll and who put in a good word for me when he needed a replacement for my predecessor.'

'What happened to your predecessor?'

'He was fired,' said Chris, with a grimace. '*Ocean Wanderer* isn't registered in Australia and she doesn't have an all-Aussie crew, so the unions don't have any say if somebody gets the boot. Captain Carroll is God on this ship. He does all the hiring and firing. Anyone who breaks his rules has only themselves to blame if they find themselves put ashore at the next port of call and replaced with someone who will toe the Captain's line.

Don't get me wrong: I like him. A good captain has to be a martinet.'

'I should have thought it was the owner who was God and the Captain his chief archangel,' said Cassandra, as they waded out of the sea. 'Surely if a captain upset an owner, he could find himself out of a job?'

'In general, yes—that's true,' he agreed. 'But I think Mr Dennison's aware that he's lucky to have Nick Carroll as his skipper. Dennison doesn't know port from starboard. Maybe he's not in the same league as Arab sheiks and Asian bankers, but he's a very rich guy and he bought the yacht on a whim. At any rate, that's what I heard. You probably know a lot more about it than I do,' he added, as they picked up their towels and began to dry themselves.

Cassandra smiled and shook her head. 'I had supper in my cabin last night. I haven't even met my sister's fiancé yet.'

'Your sister's fiancé?' Chris repeated, looking surprised. 'She and Dennison are engaged? When did that happen?'

'Weeks ago . . . before they left Vancouver.'

She was about to add that when they arrived in Sydney they were going to be married there, but he interrupted her, saying, 'Really? They're keeping it mighty quiet. Everyone thought——' He stopped short, looking slightly uncomfortable.

'Everyone thought?' she prompted.

He gave a sheepish shrug. 'You can't really blame them for putting the wrong construction on it. There is a pretty wide age gap between your sister and Mr Dennison. We thought they were just good friends, as the saying goes.'

'It's amazing how ready people are always to think the worst. My sister and Mr Dennison may have decided not to announce their engagement officially yet, but I've known about it for some time. Otherwise I shouldn't be here as his guest,' she answered firmly.

Chris gave her a thoughtful look. 'No, I can believe that,' he said. 'You're not what I was expecting.'

'What were you expecting?'

'More of a swinger, I guess. Now that I look at you more closely, I believe you might even be one of that vanishing species which my mother is always looking out for—a real, old-fashioned nice girl,' he said teasingly. 'Actually nice girls could be due for a revival, what with the herpes scare and the fact that the singles scene hasn't turned out to be as much fun as people thought. How are things over in Britain? Are people there changing their ideas?'

'I think the pendulum is beginning to swing back a bit—as it always does,' she said cautiously. 'I don't believe we're entering an age of oppressive prudery like the Victorian reaction to the lax moral climate of the Regency period. I don't think those harsh, narrow morals could ever come back.'

'I'm not so sure about that. Look how the missionaries managed to change the moral climate here in Hawaii,' said Chris. 'They didn't only put a stop to the sexual freedom of the Hawaiians. They clamped down on singing and dancing, and they even made them cut out surfing. That's something you've got to try— surfing, I mean. I'm not too good at it yet, but it has to be one of the greatest sensations in the world. You should see Nick Carroll go on his board. He took me and a couple of the crew up the coast, past Kapalua, the other day. He's better than good. He could be a professional if he wanted.'

'I'm not sure I would like a go at surfing,' said Cassandra, as they boarded the dinghy. 'But I should like to learn to snorkel.'

'That's no problem. There's plenty of gear on board. I can teach you. How about this afternoon? I'm off duty from two until six.'

'I think my sister may have some plans for this afternoon, Chris. But it's nice of you to offer.'

'Some other time, then. The reef at Black Rock by the Sheraton Hotel is a good place and so is Kapulua Bay.'

This time it was Olaf who ran down the boarding ladder as they drew near the yacht and gave Cassandra a hand to step from the dinghy to the platform.

'Thank you.' She gave him a smile which was still lingering on her lips when she reached deck level.

It faded abruptly at the sight of Captain Carroll standing almost at the same spot where he had used her towel to dry his long limbs and powerful torso less than twelve hours ago.

Now he was wearing his uniform, but a vivid recollection of being lifted bodily from the sea and, for a few seconds, held as close as if he were about to embrace her, brought a bright blush to her cheeks.

'Enjoyed your first dip in the Pacific, Miss Vernon?' he asked, with the first smile she had received from him. But there was more mockery than warmth in it.

'Yes, thank you, Captain—very much.' She cleared a constriction in her throat with a nervous cough and, striving for self-possession, added, 'Where I come from, even in summer the sea is never anything like as warm as it is here.'

He glanced at his watch. 'Your sister came back on board a few minutes ago. You have time for a shower before lunch is served at one o'clock.'

Had they been alone, she would have been strongly tempted to salute and say 'Yes, sir. Thank you, sir' in the manner of a Navy midshipman being dismissed from the presence of his commanding officer.

But however much she resented Captain Carroll's manner towards her, she wasn't prepared to go as far as being openly insubordinate in front of Olaf and Chris.

The kind of retorts she might make if he took that

tone with her the next time they were alone was another matter.

In her shower she rinsed the salt water from her hair and skin and pondered what to wear for lunch. She had the impression that, as he had yesterday, Harley Dennison was spending all day at the golf course. So it wouldn't matter too much if she wore the old tee-shirt and shorts she had put on earlier. Rosalind wouldn't approve of them, but it was the other passengers, not the officers and crew, whose opinions concerned her, and they hadn't arrived yet. Who were they? Cassandra wondered.

She had rather hoped to have Rosalind to herself some of the time. They had such a lot of catching up to do. Six years was a long time to be separated from one's only sister and although they had kept in touch by letter, it wasn't the same as seeing each other regularly.

All the time she was blow-drying her hair, her ears were alert for Rosalind's tap on the door. But by two minutes to one her sister hadn't come to collect her and, conscious of disappointment, Cassandra went on deck alone.

She found Rosalind in conversation with a short, stocky officer with a moustache. The Captain and Chris and two other men formed a separate group.

'You've been swimming, I hear,' said Rosalind, her blue gaze assessing the younger girl's appearance as she approached them. 'Come and meet Hugh Davis, the First Officer. Hugh, this is my sister Cassandra.'

'Hello, Cassandra. Welcome aboard.'

The First Officer was an Australian in his mid-forties. Clearly he took her for several years younger than she was. His manner was that of a kindly middle-aged man greeting a late-teens girl who might be shy of meeting strangers.

'Thank you, Mr Davis,' she said, smiling at him, aware that silence had fallen among the other four men.

'You've met the Captain. Let me introduce the rest of my colleagues.' Taking her by the arm, he led her towards the others who, from standing in a close circle, moved to form an open semi-circle.

'This is George Hendricks who keeps the engines in order,' he said, indicating an even older man with thick grey hair and a beard to match.

'How do you do, Mr Hendricks,' she said, as they shook hands, his grip almost making her wince.

'How are you?' The Engineer's accent was broad, his nod unsmiling yet somehow indicative of friendliness.

'And this is Terry Anson, our Radio Officer,' continued Hugh Davis, turning towards a ginger-haired man about Rosalind's age.

'Pleased to meet you, Miss Vernon.' It was difficult to place the Radio Officer's place of origin.'

'As there are now two Miss Vernons on board, I think it would be simpler if everyone called me Cassandra,' she said, after exchanging a less bone-crushing handshake with him.

At this point Atu appeared beside the Captain. 'Lunch is served, sir.'

'Thank you. Will you sit beside me, Cassandra?'

As the First Officer had a few moments earlier, Captain Carroll took her lightly by the arm and steered her in the direction of the dining saloon, which now had its windows open and folding doors pushed aside to connect it with the lounge area.

Had she given it any thought, she might have anticipated that, as a new arrival and in the absence of any more important passengers, she would be seated next to him, at least for this one meal. But she had been thinking of other things and it came as a surprise, not a welcome one. She would have preferred to find herself between the First Officer and Chris for lunch.

Atu had the chair on the right of the Captain's place pulled out for her. She was glad when Nick Carroll removed his long brown fingers from her arm. She had found the contact, casual as it was, curiously disturbing. Indeed everything about the man, his voice, the enigmatic expression on his face in repose, his whole physical presence, made her uneasy.

The others had been having pre-lunch drinks which they had brought to the table with them. Rosalind, she noticed, had an exotic concoction in a tall glass with a straw. All the men except the one on her left were drinking beer. The Captain's glass appeared to contain nothing but water with some ice floating in it, and the water glasses beside each place were being filled with cold water by one of the two stewards assisting Atu.

'Would you care for something more interesting than water, Cassandra?' the First Officer, who was on her right, enquired. 'Your sister is having a Mai Tai, but I think you might find that rather potent. A Chi Chi is a drink which a lot of ladies enjoy. It doesn't have more than a dash of vodka in it if you'd rather not drink too much alcohol at midday.'

At least he didn't seem to assume that she must be a swinger, she thought gratefully. That he and all the men round the table, except Chris who now knew the truth, regarded her sister as a gold-digging adventuress made her cringe.

'I never drink spirits at all,' she answered candidly. 'Although I do like wine sometimes. Can a Chi Chi be made without vodka? What else is in it?'

'It's a mixture of lemon and pineapple juice with coconut milk and crushed ice,' Hugh Davis told her. 'The vodka gives it a kick, but it isn't essential.' He passed her request to a steward.

Throughout the first part of the meal, which began with a crabmeat quiche followed by a fish called *mahi mahi* baked in vermouth with macadamia nuts, he continued to make pleasant small-talk.

Although he had made a point of putting her next to

him, Captain Carroll made very little effort to be
sociable. From time to time the First Officer included
him and the Engineer, sitting opposite her, in the
conversation, They would then contribute a remark or
two. But for the most part both men were noticeably
taciturn compared with the affable Sydneysider—
which, he told her, was what the natives of that city
were called.

However, although neither of them had much to say,
she had the feeling that it was only the Engineer who
for most of the meal was deep in his own thoughts.
Intuition told her that the Captain was giving the
conversation his close attention and that every word she
uttered was being weighed, and perhaps found wanting.

Several times she glanced in his direction to find that
piercing grey gaze focused on her as she answered the
First Officer's questions. Not knowing what her sister
might have told them about her family background and
the reason why they hadn't seen each other for years,
she was reluctant to say anything which might not tally
with Rosalind's version. Perhaps Hugh Davis didn't
realise she was being evasive, but she felt sure the
Captain was aware of it.

At the other end of the table, her sister was carrying
on a separate conversation with the two youngest
officers. Cassandra had expected that Rosalind would
be opposite her in the chair now occupied by the
Engineer. But although the Captain's subordinates had
waited for her to choose where she wanted to sit before
taking their places, she had selected the place furthest
from Cassandra. But not for that reason, probably. It
was also the furthest away from 'Captain Bligh' whom,
clearly, she disliked as much as he disliked her.

'How long has this island been popular with tourists,
Captain Carroll?' she asked, after Atu had placed a
bowl of fruit salad in front of her.

'The Sixties were the beginning of it. Discriminating

Canadians were the ones who put Maui on the map, and then people from Alaska began to spend pipeline money here.'

'The place has been ruined, if you ask me,' was the Engineer's sudden gruff comment. He had refused the fruit salad and now he pushed back his chair. 'You'll excuse me, Captain . . . Miss Cassandra . . .' He left the table.

She was charmed by the old-fashioned courtesy of the way he addressed her. When he had gone, she said, 'Mr Hendrickson isn't an Australian, is he?' She thought her ear had detected a slight difference between his accent and that of the First Officer.

'No, George is a Kiwi . . . a New Zealander,' he told her. 'We're a mixed bunch aboard *Ocean Wanderer*. Now there's a country you must see while you're in the southern hemisphere—New Zealand. To my mind it's one of the most beautiful places on earth.'

'I'd like to see it very much, but unfortunately I shan't have time. I have to go back to England and earn my living.'

'What is your occupation?' The question came from the man on her left.

'At the moment I haven't one,' she admitted reluctantly.

'Then why must you go back to Britain? Why not see how you like living in a better climate?' suggested the First Officer.

'Aren't there restrictions on people going to live in Australia and New Zealand?' she asked him.

Before he could answer, the Captain said, 'Indeed there are, and they favour immigrants with useful qualifications. I don't think Cassandra would stand much chance of being allowed in without any specialised skills. Although many Australians are of British descent, in the past two or three decades some of the immigrants from Britain have made themselves pretty unpopular. Whingeing poms, they're known as. To whinge being Australian slang for to gripe and groan incessantly,' he added sardonically.

His thinly veiled antagonsim was beginning to get to her.

'And I strike you as a potential whinger, do I, Captain?' she asked, with a sparkle in her eyes.

'I didn't say that ... merely that some of your compatriots have that unfortunate tendency,' was his cool response. 'I'll have coffee in my quarters, Atu. Would you excuse me, Miss Vernon?'

As the Engineer had before him, the Captain rose from his place and left the table.

From behind his shoulders looked even broader than from a frontal view. As he walked away she found herself studying the way his back tapered to a lean waist. His white shorts were short and close-fitting, outlining his hard male backside and exposing the backs of his thighs, only lightly furred with dark hair. Below the turned-down tops of his immaculate stockings, muscular calves stretched the knitted fabric. But his ankles were slimmer and more elegant than those of his officers. There was no denying his physical magnetism. In that respect she had reluctantly to admit that he came very close to personifying her idea of a supremely attractive man. But his personality didn't match his good looks. In *that* respect she found him extremely dislikeable; critical, sarcastic, cold.

'How long are we staying here, Hugh?' she asked.

'At least until the weekend when some more guests arrive, and then possibly most of next week to give them time to look around this area before we move on to the other end of the island where the terrain is different.'

'How many passengers can *Ocean Wanderer* carry?'

'There are eight double cabins apart from the owner's

suite. It's not often they're all occupied, but I understand they will be for our Christmas cruise through the Yasawas. They're a group of small Fijian islands, one of which is Atu's home island, so we always get a special welcome there.'

Although she found him a pleasant companion, the person Cassandra was longing to talk to was her sister. But Rosalind seemed in no hurry to break off her chat with the two younger men.

Since the Captain's departure their conversation had become noticeably livelier. From snatches she overheard, Cassandra had the impression that Ros was flirting with them. With her coffee she was sipping another Mai Tai. Remembering what Hugh had said about them, Cassandra wondered if it was the second potent drink which was making her sister behave in such a provocative way.

Most of her alluring smiles seemed to be directed at Terry Anson rather than Chris, and Terry wasn't hiding the fact that he found her desirable. Twice, as she flashed a quick, troubled glance in their direction, Cassandra saw the Radio Officer give her sister an openly undressing look. She hoped Hugh wasn't aware of what was going on nearby.

Perhaps he was. The next time there was a break in the others' conversation, he said to them, 'I'm sure Rosalind and Cassandra must be looking forward to a private chat, and the rest of us have things to do.'

He rose to his feet, giving a clear intimation to the two junior officers that they were to leave the table.

When the men had gone, Rosalind said, 'Let's go and relax under the awning.'

Drink in hand, she led the way to the lounge area where she curled on a white-cushioned sofa.

'I'm sorry I wasn't around when you woke up. I had an appointment to have my legs waxed and I thought you'd sleep most of the morning.'

'Ros, is there somewhere where we could talk privately?'

'Why not here? The stewards have almost finished.' Rosalind looked towards the dining saloon where Atu and his assistants were clearing the table.

'It's not very private here. We could be overheard by someone on the deck below. I think my cabin would be better,' said Cassandra.

Her sister looked puzzled; but after a moment she shrugged and uncurled herself. 'If you've something that private to say we'll go to mine. I can get ready to sunbathe while you lay bare your dark secrets.'

It wasn't a surprise to Cassandra to find herself, a short time later, in what was recognisably the owner's suite. From the luxuriously appointed private sitting-room, Rosalind took herself into an adjoining large stateroom furnished with a king-size double bed.

Her sister unfastened her sandals and kicked them off, leaving them lying on the champagne-coloured carpet.

'I hope it doesn't shock you to find that Harley and I sleep together,' she remarked, unzipping her shorts. 'Or have you managed to grow up with reasonably up-to-date ideas in spite of Father's puritanical influence?'

'I think so.' Cassandra watched her wriggle the shorts over her hips and, when they had dropped round her feet, step out of them, leaving them there.

Rosalind started unbuttoning her shirt. 'I suppose, shut up with Father all this time, you haven't had many boy-friends.'

'I haven't had any,' the younger girl answered. 'But I haven't lost the chance. I'm still only twenty. There's time.'

'Yes, but what a waste of those years! Never mind: it's all over now and you can start having a good time. But don't let young Chris try to coax you into a fling with him. He's as randy as hell. They all are—even Captain Bligh.'

'I don't know about the Captain, but it's fairly obvious the Radio Officer is,' Cassandra said dryly. 'Ros, when I mentioned to Chris this morning that I hadn't yet met your fiancé, he didn't know you were engaged. Don't you think you should wear your ring at times? To make it clear you are Harley's future wife, not just . . . a temporary companion?'

Her sister rummaged in a drawer and brought out a handful of blue cotton crochet. 'There is no ring,' she said flatly. 'I made that up on the spur of the moment. I didn't want you to start making a fuss. In fact I hoped it wouldn't be necessary to have a showdown for some time. But as Chris has let the cat out of the bag . . .' She stopped and gave an irritable sigh. 'I told you a white lie, Cass, but I did it with the best of intentions. I was afraid if you knew the real set-up, you wouldn't come.'

Cassandra stared at her, appalled. At length she said, in a low voice, 'Do you love him?'

Rosalind was adjusting the minimal bikini which was what the two wisps of crochet had turned out to be.

'No, I don't love him,' she answered. 'But I'd marry him tomorrow if he asked me. He's a kind, generous man who's treated me better than any of the other men I've known.'

Cassandra felt as if she had been punched in the stomach. Coming at the end of a long period of stress, and at a time when her whole system was thrown out of balance by jet-lag, a shock of this order was hard to take calmly.

She said, 'You're right: I wouldn't have come—and I can't possibly stay. I shouldn't feel comfortable. I—I don't know how you can be.'

Her sister's blue eyes flashed angrily. She put her hands on her hips and, standing with arms akimbo, she snapped, 'Before you start taking a holier-than-thou attitude, just you listen to me for a minute! While you've been living in your ivory tower in Cambridge,

I've been out in the world; and, believe me, it's a bloody tough world for a girl on her own. You think you've had a hard time looking after Father, but it's been no picnic for me since he threw me out. I was pregnant. You didn't know that, did you? I sneaked out to a party one night and somebody's idea of fun was to make the drinks extra strong, and the next thing I knew I was preggo. It happens all the time,' she added bitterly. 'Girls of that age pretend they know all the answers, but half of them don't and a lot of them still get caught.'

'Ros ... I had no idea. How terrible for you!' Cassandra exclaimed.

'Oh, well, it's a long time ago, and I survived,' the older girl said, with a shrug. 'But whatever Father suffered at the end, I think he had it coming to him,' she went on coldly. 'What kind of man, when his daughter goes to him for help, tells her to get lost?'

'What did you do? Why did you keep the truth from me?' Cassandra asked.

'I thought you might be as disgusted with me as he was. You were only fourteen and you hadn't begun to be interested in boys. I thought you'd be ashamed of me,' Rosalind told her.

'Oh, no—I loved you. I should have wanted to help you. What about the baby's father? Wouldn't he help?'

Rosalind's pretty face took on a hostile expression which Cassandra's intuition told her was a mask to hide the unhealed sense of humiliation which her sister still felt when she was forced to remember that period of her life.

'I'd been dancing and fooling around with two or three boys at that party. It could have been any one of them—and none of them was the type to admit to being responsible. From what little I remember about it, any of them may have——' Her lower lip quivered. 'I hate men the ...! I hate the whole bloody lot of them.'

'They're not all like that, Ros.'

'Aren't they? What would you know about it?—a

twenty-year-old virgin who's never had anything to do with them.' Rosalind put out her cigarette with a series of angry jabs. 'What did I do with my drink?' she said, looking round for it. 'How about you?' she asked, brandishing the glass.

'No, thanks. Not at the moment. What really happened after you left home?' she said. 'In your letters you made it sound as if you were enjoying being independent. Was all that made up for my benefit?'

'No, I liked living in London. The job in the dress shop was true and the bedsitter in Fulham was true. I was lucky. Things worked out quite well—except that I wasn't able to get rid of the baby. I had to have it.'

Cassandra's eyes widened. 'You've got a child? Where?'

'Somewhere in England, I suppose. She was adopted—I couldn't have kept her. It's impossible to bring up a kid on your own without any help. So I did the best thing for her . . . gave her away to people who could look after her properly.'

Cassandra wasn't deceived by her sister's expressionless statement of the facts. She could only begin to guess at the anguish Rosalind or any girl in that situation must suffer in making that irreversible decision.

'That's as much of my life story as I'm going to tell you today,' her sister said, with sudden impatience. 'The rest can wait. I want to catch a sunbathe before we go shopping in Lahaina. What kind of swimsuit were you wearing this morning? Straps or a halter?'

'Straps. I only have one suit.'

'Then you'd better borrow one of mine, with a halter. If you don't take care to alternate them, especially at the beginning, you don't get a nice even tan on your shoulders without marks.'

Cassandra looked doubtfully at the bikini her sister was wearing. It was little more than a G-string and two

small triangles of crochet. She knew she would feel uncomfortable with her figure exposed to that extent—particularly if Captain Carroll should happen to walk by.

'Have you one a bit more covered up? I'm so white at
the moment—it makes me feel self-conscious.'

'You won't get brown by covering up.' Rosalind
opened the drawer from which she had taken her bikini.
'Here you are, how about this?'—offering her sister a
crimson and violet bikini which did look relatively
modest.

However, when she put it on she discovered that,
although there was more of it, the design was extremely
sexy. Like the dress which Rosalind had chosen for her
yesterday, the swimsuit wasn't her style.

'Look, I'm not sure I should have another sunbathe
today, or at least not until later on when the sun is less
strong.'

'Ten minutes with plenty of oil on won't roast you,'
her sister said firmly.

Cassandra was still reluctant to appear in public in a
halter which moulded her breasts into jutting cones
instead of their natural round shape. It was the kind of
bikini worn by actresses and dancers wanting to be
photographed; not by retiring girls such as herself.

'Don't you wear a cover-up to go on deck?' she asked.

'What for? This isn't a hotel. We're only going as far
as the foredeck.'

Which was in full view of the bridge, Cassandra
remembered with dismay. Then she realised there was
no reason why the Captain should be on the bridge in
the early afternoon with the ship at anchor. He was
probably still in his quarters, wherever they were.

Some time later, after lying on her back for five
minutes and on her front for another five, she
retreated into the circle of shade cast by a striped
sunbrella, one of two in the area surrounding the
splash pool.

Absentmindedly admiring the sleek contours of her sister's beautiful, glistening body stretched on a towel-covered sun-bed, Cassandra confronted the greatest problem of her life.

The decision to devote herself to her father when even his doctor had been in favour of having him put in a hospital had been clear-cut and simple compared with the dilemma which faced her now.

Whether she would find Harley Dennison a pleasant man or an objectionable one was not germane to the fundamental issue. Whatever he was like, he was keeping Ros as his mistress with, at present, no intention of regularising their relationship. That made her sister a woman who, although not the social outcast she would have been a century earlier, was still *persona non grata* among a great many people.

How could it be otherwise?

The sordid connotations of her sister's present lifestyle made Cassandra feel sick and disgusted. She wished she had never come; never found out the shaming truth.

At the same time she recognised the force of Rosalind's retort that her own sequestered life in Cambridge had kept her in ignorance of the harsher realities of the world at large.

Lacking the sympathetic handling of two affectionate parents, Ros had made a bad start in life. Was it any wonder that, given her unstable nature, her life was still in a mess?

And the fact remains that I love her, Cassandra mused. I can't go off and leave her without at least trying to make her see that there are other options for her. I must get her out of this somehow. But to do that means staying on board and having everyone think I'm from the same mould as Ros. Nick Carroll already thinks that ... he's made it clear he has nothing but contempt for either of us. Just for a short time, before lunch, he was polite and made me sit next to him, but it didn't last long. Before lunch was over he was sniping at me. Can I blame him? What would I think in his place?

Mindful of his warning that it could be dangerous to doze in the sun, and remembering that Ros had had three strong drinks, she stood up and moved to where her sister was lying. Tanned as she was, it was possible she could burn if she lay too long in these still-fierce rays burning down from a cloudless sky.

'I'm going below, Ros. Don't fall asleep, will you?'

Rosalind's response was a drowsy murmur. She sounded half asleep already. Cassandra shook her more vigorously until she rolled over, saying, in a disgruntled tone, 'What's the matter?'

'Sorry to disturb you. I'm going to my cabin and I didn't want you to fall asleep and get burned.'

'I never burn.' Rosalind raised the end of the sun-bed into a backrest and reached for her cigarettes. 'I'll have another half hour and then I'll get ready to go ashore.'

As Cassandra left her, she was exhaling smoke. Her sister couldn't help thinking that all this smoking and drinking couldn't be good for her looks, which, on her present course, were her principal asset.

Cassandra was pattering along the starboard walkway, wondering what chance she had of persuading Ros to abandon her current way of life, when Nick Carroll came into view.

At first he didn't notice her because he was strolling towards the rails, crossing her path at an angle. Instinctively she slowed, unwilling for him to see her in the arresting bikini which drew attention to her unattractive whiteness in a place where everyone else was beautifully bronzed.

However, when he stopped by the rails and rested his hands on the top bar, looking towards the two other large islands not far from Maui, she knew it was unlikely she could sidle round the corner of the saloon without being spotted.

In profile his features were even more dominating than from a full-face view. The large nose, the jutting chin, the prominent slant of his cheekbones combined to form an impression of a strong, forceful, even ruthless personality. Yet, as her mind registered that impression, she was also aware that it was a distinguished profile with a high forehead and finely formed nostrils and lips. His neck was long. He had nice ears.

When the Australian suddenly swung to face her, she made a nervous movement which was almost, but not quite, a recoil.

Certainly it was because she was annoyed with herself for showing that he made her nervous that she went to the other extreme and forced herself to join him at the rails, asking, 'What are those islands called?'

'That one is Molokai, where a famous priest called Father Damien devoted himself to looking after the lepers who used to be sent there,' he told her, indicating the larger island. 'The one to the south of it is Lanai. It's a plantation island owned by the Dole Pineapple Company.'

'So they're both untouched by tourism?'

'Molokai is open to visitors, but not many go there. Whether it will stay that way is doubtful unless the planning authorities take a much firmer stand against rapacious developers than they have in the past.'

He removed his gaze from the steep, deeply-fissured mountainsides of the island some miles away and turned it on her, his dark grey eyes flicking briefly over her slender figure and the contours exposed by her sister's pin-up style bikini.

'But many people like to have shops and discos and a wide choice of restaurants when they come on holiday,' he went on. 'The trouble is that you can't have all those amenities and retain peace and quiet.'

Cassandra thought it highly likely that Rosalind would consider shops and nightclubs essential, but neither was high on her own list of priorities, and it irked her that he should assume things about her without attempting to find out what kind of person she was.

For a reason she couldn't define, it was important to her to disabuse this man of the idea that she was the empty-headed, flighty little 'swinger' which they all—not only Chris—appeared to have been expecting.

'It seems lovely here to me, even if it is a bit more built up than I expected. Coming from England, in November, I find all this brilliance and warmth, and the wonderful flowers, even lovelier than I expected. You're used to it, of course, and perhaps you tend to notice only the changes for the worse, as one does on one's home ground. There's a lot about Cambridge which hasn't improved in my lifetime. But in a good summer the Backs—the college gardens running down to the river—are still amazingly beautiful.'

Without thinking, as she was talking, she had propped her elbows on the top bar behind her and rested one foot on the bottom rail. It wasn't intended to be a provocative pose, but it seemed he took it as one. Again his cool gaze travelled downwards, making her sharply aware thet her posture threw out her chest and, unintentionally, drew attention to her breasts and navel.

Nick Carroll's appraisal was not the slow lustful leer which, several times during lunch, the Radio Officer had directed at Rosalind. It wasn't a leer at all.

They're all as randy as hell—even Captain Bligh, her sister had told her.

But however long it had been since the man beside her had held a woman in his arms, his desires were considerably less inflammable than those of his amorous subordinate. The expression on his face seemed to say that if she wanted to flaunt herself she

was free to do so, but she was wasting her time with
him. She wasn't his type.

Quickly she put her foot back on the deck and
removed her elbows from the bar. At that moment she
would have given a great deal to be covered from neck
to knee by the converted dress shirt.

She would have excused herself and hurried away,
but he said, 'You grew up in Cambridge? I had the idea
you and your sister came from London.'

'Ros worked in London for a time, but I've never
lived anywhere but in Cambridge. My father was a
don—a professor at one of the colleges,' she added
explanatorily, although it surprised her to find herself
telling him these personal details. 'He died a few weeks
ago.'

And your mother?'

'I never knew her, and my sister has only faint
memories of her.' She was already regretting telling him
even these few facts. 'If you'll excuse me, I have to go
and get changed.'

But when she would have walked away, he forced her
to linger by saying, 'Have you other sisters and
brothers?'

She shook her head.

'How old are you, Cassandra?'

'I'm twenty.'

'You look younger—too young to be on your own in
the world.'

'I'm not on my own, Captain Carroll. I have a very
dear sister,' she replied, with a level look. 'Although we
haven't seen much of each other just recently, we've
always been very close, Ros and I. Being four years
older, she was almost like a mother to me when we were
children. I could never feel alone in the world with my
sister to turn to.'

The fiercely angry reaction she was prepared to let
loose if, by so much as the lift of an eyebrow, he

showed what he thought of her sister, was never put to the test.

His expression remained inscrutable. He made no comment on her statement. His reply was, 'There's no need to keep calling me Captain Carroll. My name is Nicholas ... generally shortened to Nick.'

With a slight nod, he turned away, leaving her free to go below.

On closer inspection, Lahaina seemed to Cassandra to retain considerable character in spite of too many shops selling tawdry souvenirs and too many tourists seeking things to take home.

From an open downstairs window of the Pioneer Inn, the hotel she had noticed yesterday, came the strum of a guitar and the pleasant voice of a young man singing to people in the bar. At the other end of the building she caught a glimpse of a dining-room where, later, some of the diners would eat their meal sitting in high-backed wing chairs whose shabby, sun-faded covers gave the room a down-at-heel charm.

Today, being less tired than yesterday, she was better able to resist her sister's attempts to make her buy things she didn't like.

'I shan't need an extensive wardrobe, Ros,' she said firmly. 'A couple of cool, simple dresses to wear in the evening, and a basic minimum of beach clothes. To buy more would be a waste of money.'

They were having iced drinks in one of the café-bars on the seaward side of Front Street. The incoming tide was lapping against the pilings supporting the balustrade beside their table. At another table a man in a yellow singlet and a blue baseball cap was focusing his camera on *Ocean Wanderer* while his friend and their wives speculated about the yacht's ownership.

Rosalind listened in to some of their conversation before she returned her attention to her sister. It was clear to Cassandra that Ros had got a big kick from their envious remarks. Perhaps it was because, at rock bottom, she had no real confidence in herself that she found it satisfying to be part of a rich man's entourage and to bask in reflected prestige.

'Listen, Cass, I didn't have to invite you to join us. But you're my sister and I didn't like the idea of your being on your own, especially at Christmas. But if you're going to make snide remarks all the time, I could begin to regret asking you out here.'

'Did you really expect me to take the situation in my stride?' Cassandra countered.

'No, perhaps not. As you've spent your entire life with Father, it would be surprising if some of his narrow attitudes hadn't rubbed off on you. But he's dead and you're here, and you're just going to have to accept that I'm living my life my way. It's not for you to sit in moral judgment.'

Cassandra knew this wasn't the time or the place to try to persuade Ros to see that her way was a path which, as her looks deteriorated, could only lead downhill.

She said, 'You can't expect me to be happy about accepting Mr Dennison's hospitality.'

'I don't see why not. He knows it makes me happy to have you here—or it would if you'd stop being so bloody censorious. Nobody's asking *you* to do anything immoral, for heaven's sake!'

It seemed to Cassandra that, in this last remark, there was a tacit admission that Ros wasn't entirely comfortable with her role as Harley's girl-friend. If that was the case, there was hope that, given time, she could be persuaded to give it up.

Later, when they were back on board and she was alone in her cabin, preparing for her first encounter with the man who was keeping her sister, Cassandra spent some time thoughtfully re-examining her motives for deciding to stay on the yacht.

How much was she influenced by the fact that if she returned to England now she would be giving up weeks of luxurious living in a wonderful climate for a solitary existence in a dismal bedsitter at a time of year when grey skies and rain were the norm?

On the other hand, to remain was to put herself in the position of being thought to condone her sister's relationship. They might not show it, but she would be constantly aware that Nicholas Carroll, most of his officers and some if not all the other guests had a low opinion of both Vernon girls.

At the end of her deliberations, when it was almost time to go on deck, she had come to the conclusion that if she went back to Europe it would be the end between her and her sister. If she stayed there was a chance they would salvage the strong affection which had once bound them. Surely to recover that was worth a try, no matter what the cost in private humiliation?

Nevertheless it was with great reluctance that she left her cabin and made her way up to the lounge deck to meet Harley Dennison.

CHAPTER THREE

HE was not as bad as she expected. Neither as old or as vulgar nor as overtly lecherous in his manner towards her sister as Cassandra's worrying preconception of him.

In reality the yacht's owner was a burly man in his middle fifties, carrying a good deal of superfluous weight round his middle but otherwise healthy and active-looking. In his younger days his hair must have been as fair and thick as hers. Now what remained was still fair with some grey around his ears.

She liked his sense of humour. It was difficult to dislike anyone whose eyes twinkled as often and who laughed as readily as Harley Dennison.

She soon realised that the image of a rather crude and unpleasant self-made man which she had had in her mind was an inaccurate picture. Perhaps he was ruthless, even unscrupulous, in his business dealings—and she didn't yet know how he had amassed the fortune which enabled him, on a whim, to buy a multi-million-dollar vessel—but in private life he was one of the most cheerful, relaxed men she had ever met.

They did not, as she expected, dine on board but at a restaurant called Pineapple Hill, which was close to the eighteen-hole Arnold Palmer championship golf course where Harley spent most of his time. Tonight he had invited two more of his golfing acquaintances and their wives to be his guests. To make the number even, Nick Carroll had been asked to join them.

The other golfers were sharing one of the golf villas on the seven hundred and fifty-acre Kapalua Bay resort complex. They had been able to walk to the restaurant which was situated at the end of a mile-long drive bordered by tall Norfolk Island pines.

Harley and his party had arrived by car. Had they gone in a taxi, probably Nick would have sat in front with the driver and Cassandra would have shared the back seat with her sister and her host. But it seemed that wherever they berthed for any length of time, he always rented a car in which to get about on shore. With him at the wheel and Ros beside him, Cassandra had found herself sharing the back seat with Nick.

Tonight he was wearing civilian clothes. But the fact that his long legs were hidden by tropic-weight trousers and his sinewy forearms by the sleeves of a silk tweed blazer had not made her less aware of the powerful masculine body sitting beside her as they retraced the route to the airport and then drove beyond it into a part of the island she hadn't seen before and where she had her first sight of a low-growing spiky grey-green crop which she realised were pineapple plants.

Throughout the meal she had been separated from Nick by the two golfers and their wives, both of whom plied him with many questions about other parts of the Pacific.

At times the three of them were having a separate conversation from the three other men and the Vernon girls. Glancing down the table now and then, Cassandra noticed that Nick wasn't merely answering the two women's enquiries. He was exerting himself to be pleasant. Turning on the charm, was the phrase which came into her mind; and surprisingly potent charm it was, she realised, seeing his white teeth flash as he smiled at the elder of the wives, a rather plain, dowdy person at least twenty years his senior.

Although seated far beyond the range of his smile, Cassandra was startled to find it had an effect on her.

She found herself wondering what her reaction would be in the most unlikely event that he should smile directly at her, all the coldness swept from his face by the sudden warm, friendly grin.

Perhaps with people he liked he wasn't the sardonic autocrat he had seemed to her so far.

It was on the way back to Lahaina that, after chaffing Rosalind about her resistance to any form of physical exertion, Harley said, over his shoulder, 'How about you, Cassandra? Are you as lazy as this sister of yours? Or are you into exercise?'

'At home I usually went for a fairly energetic walk every morning before breakfast,' she answered.

'You can do that here, if you get up before the sun's up. Nick jogs around town every morning. He'll take you over with him if you want to keep up your walks.'

'Oh, no ... it isn't important ... here I'll be swimming instead,' she said hurriedly. She felt sure Nick didn't want to be forced to ferry her ashore with him.

'Swimming is good exercise, but it doesn't have the same cardio-vascular benefits as brisk walking or running,' was his unexpected comment. 'You're welcome to come ashore with me if half-six isn't too early for you—and you're punctual,' he added.

'It isn't too early ... but are you sure you don't mind?' she said doubtfully.

'Not at all,' he said politely.

Later, before turning out her reading lamp, Cassandra set the alarm on the digital clock to wake her at half past five.

She was ready and waiting when Nick appeared and said, 'Good morning.'

His strong chin which, late last night, had begun to show a dark shadow where his beard grew, was now smooth from recent shaving. He was wearing a lighweight navy track top with white shorts, tennis socks and running shoes. He had a small terry towel with him.

Beyond exhanging the time of day, they had no conversation going ashore.

'I run for thirty minutes. I'll be back here at seven-fifteen,' he told her, at the small boat harbour, as he unzipped his top and left it with the towel in the dinghy.

She watched him stride off and soon break into a lope which became a run before he was out of sight. Stripped to the waist, his body was even more impressive. Yet for a tall, powerful man he looked very light on his feet, springing along with a lithe easy rhythm very different from the ungainly gait of some of the early morning joggers she had passed on the towpath in Cambridge.

The main part of the town was on flat ground. She decided to explore the area behind Front Street.

As she walked up and down quiet side streets laid out more or less on a grid pattern, several people at work in their gardens gave her friendly smiles. Every garden had beautiful shrubs and one had a hedge which was a mass of pale blue plumbago flowers.

Although it wasn't as hot as it would be as soon as the sun rose, the early morning temperature and the humidity level were enough to make Cassandra's tee-shirt cling damply to her back by the time she returned to the harbour.

However, when Nick reappeared her sticky condition was nothing to the state he was in. His face and body gleamed with sweat, emphasising the play of muscle under his smooth brown skin. As he came to a halt she could see rivulets trickling down his face from his now damp and tousled hair. But he seemed to have enjoyed himself. Before he picked up the towel and began to mop his glistening neck and shoulders, he actually smiled at her.

As she smiled back, she was uneasily aware that, if he

chose to be nice to her, she could learn to like this man a lot more than she would have thought possible on the day of her arrival, or during the early hours of the following day when he had told her off for swimming at night.

It wasn't the whole man who was beginning to appeal to her; merely his body and his face. About the workings of his mind—by far the most important part of anyone—she had almost no knowledge at all.

None of the serious topics which united people or divided them, such as political, religious and racial attitudes, had been touched on in the short time she had known him.

How could you like a man when you didn't begin to know what he thought about any of the issues which cemented or prevented friendship. The one thing she did know for certain was that he despised her sister. Which, even though secretly she agreed with him in deploring Rosalind's lifestyle, put them on different sides of an irremovable barrier.

On the way back to *Ocean Wanderer*, he said, 'If you can persuade your sister to take some time off from shopping when she's ashore, there are one or two things here worth seeing before we move on.'

Although irked by the dig at Ros, she said pleasantly, 'Really? What are they?'

'Just across the street from the library there's the Baldwin House, the home of a missionary and doctor who lived here in the last century.' He raked back his breeze-ruffled hair with a careless sweep of lean fingers. 'Or if you cross the main highway and go inland, up to the top of Lahainaluna Road, you can see a replica of the first printing press on the island in a small printing museum. There's also a fine view of the town from up there. It would be hot walking up. You'd do better to take the car when it's free. Have you a licence?'

She shook her head. 'We didn't need a car in

Cambridge. I should learn to drive, I suppose. Like typing and knowing how to work a computer, it's a fairly essential skill, isn't it?'

'As you say, it depends where you live, but even I—living at sea—find my licence useful at times.'

Atu had seen them approaching. He was waiting to hand her out of the dinghy. Before releasing his hold, he asked, 'Shall I lay another place for breakfast, Captain?'

Nick said, 'I have breakfast in the saloon immediately after my shower. Would you care to join me? Your sister rarely emerges from her quarters before nine or ten.'

Perhaps it wasn't meant as a reminder that Rosalind was, at this moment, in bed with a man whose only attraction for her was his extremely large income. But whether or not that was his intention, Nick's last remark made Cassandra miserably conscious of her sister's invidious standing aboard the yacht and her own share of obloquy for seeming to go along with Rosalind's behaviour and share in its benefits.

It was a painful flash of embarrassment which made her say stiffly, 'Thank you, but I've imposed myself on you quite long enough for one morning. I'll take coffee in my cabin.'

No sooner had she hurried away than she began to regret turning down the chance to continue the conversation begun on the dinghy.

He might not have wanted to share his breakfast table with her. Like Harley the night before, Atu had made it difficult for him not to do the civil thing. But whether or not he found her company a bore, she would have liked talking to him, finding out what made him tick.

Tomorrow he probably wouldn't invite her to join him. Opportunities never came twice.

He was wrong about Rosalind not putting in an appearance until halfway through the morning. She came on deck early that day. She wanted Harley to drop them at the shops at Kapalua on his way to play golf.

Had it not been for the fact that everything her sister bought in the two and a half hours she spent shopping was paid for with American dollars she could only have received from Harley, Cassandra would have enjoyed browsing with her.

The twenty or so shops surrounded a landscaped courtyard adjoining the island's best hotel.

Most of the things in the shops were in much better taste than the wares on sale in Lahaina, and there was one shop, callled Brioni, where Cassandra would have loved to have unlimited funds.

As well as high fashion clothes, Brioni sold *objets d'art*. That day there was a display of beautiful iridescent glass vases and ornaments in the area just inside the entrance. But it was when they came to the part of the showroom where the clothes were displayed that, after looking round for a few minutes, she knew these garments were 'her'. This was the look she wanted.

The designs were all very simple, and all made from natural fibres—silk, cotton and linen. The colours were neutrals—black, white, pale beige and taupe.

The prices struck her, by any standards, as exorbitant. But it didn't matter that the clothes were far out of her reach. She had found her look and could probably achieve the same effect by hunting for inexpensive separates in similar colours and shapes.

Rosalind didn't share her enthusiasm. 'In hot climates you need bright colours,' she said, as they left the shop.

'Not on everyone. We're different types, Ros. I haven't your vivid colouring. Bright colours extinguish me.'

'They wouldn't if you wore more make-up. When

that girl at the store did your eyes you looked a
different girl.'

'I know—not myself at all,' Cassandra said dryly.
'Don't try to make me over in your image, Ros. It
wouldn't work. You take after our mother and I'm
more like Aunt Esmée when she was young.'

'Yes, and look what happened to her. Nobody
showed her how to make the best of herself and she got
stuck on the shelf and died a wizened old virgin,' her
sister said scathingly, as if there could be no worse fate.

Later, when they were having a salad on the terrace
at the Bay Club, a restaurant at the southern end of
crescent-shaped Kapalua Bay, from which they could
see the outline of corals under the blue-green water,
Cassandra asked, 'Is Harley a widower?'

'Divorced. He and his wife hadn't been getting along
for years. When all the children were grown-up, they
split. She's remarried now. Harley says he won't ever
remarry. But I may be able to change his mind about
that.'

Cassandra waited until an attentive waiter had
refilled their glasses before she said, 'Have you given up
hope of falling in love with a nice man and living the
rest of your life with him?'

'Cass, that whole concept is a pipedream for
schoolgirls and tired housewives. It doesn't happen in
real life. People think they're falling in love, but it's
only chemistry. I know what I want out of life—and it
isn't a mortgage and two kids and a husband who falls
asleep watching television.'

'What do you want?'

'Nice clothes. Places like this'—with a gesture
encompassing the restaurant and its spectacular view of
a shimmering sea and the haze-veiled outlines of
Molokai and Lanai.

'But you won't always be twenty-four. What happens
when you're thirty-four . . . forty-four?'

'I'll worry about my forties when I come to them. I might never get there,' Rosalind answered cheerfully.

It wasn't the time or the place to launch another argument with her. Cassandra felt that the first thing she had to do was to re-establish a strong rapport with her sister. Which wasn't going to be easy when they held such divergent views on certain fundamental concepts. But perhaps this conversation over lunch had been a beginning.

Later, thinking over her sister's remarks during lunch, she found herself wondering if Nick Carroll shared the view that love never lasted, and that was why he was still single. Perhaps, like Harley's, his past included a marriage which hadn't worked out and had ended in divorce.

I must find out from Mrs Shane, she thought. And then: What has his past—or future—to do with me? He's someone I shall never meet again once this trip is over.

Cassandra discovered the Upstart Crow, a combination of bookshop and café, the day before Harley's other guests were due to fly in.

It was part of a timbered shopping complex called The Wharf, on the opposite side of the street from the banyan tree and the Pioneer Inn. After browsing for some time and treating herself to a couple of paperbacks, she bought a cup of coffee and took it to one of the tables on the balcony outside the shop's doorway.

She was dipping into one of her new books when a familiar voice said, 'Aren't the books in your cabin the kind you enjoy?'

Looking up into Nick Carroll's dark grey eyes, she felt a strange leap of the heart.

'Oh . . . hello.'

They had been going ashore together every morning

since the first time, but had had little conversation, and
he hadn't repeated the invitation to breakfast with him.

She surprised herself by smiling and saying, 'Have
you time to join me for a coffee?'

For a moment or two he considered the suggestion. She
wondered if she were going to be courteously snubbed.

Then he nodded. 'I have time.'

She indicated the chair beside hers and rose to go
into the shop. 'You like your coffee black, without
sugar, I believe?'

'Yes—' he laid a restraining hand on her bare arm,
'—but I'll get it.' He glanced at her mug from which as
yet she had taken only two sips of the very hot coffee.
'You haven't tried one of their cakes. They're good. I'm
going to have one. Shall I bring one for you?'

Cassandra didn't normally eat cake, but the ones on
the coffee counter had looked as if they might be home-
made, without too much sugar in them. She had no
great liking for sweet things.

'Thank you . . . but this isn't fair. I invited you to be
my guest.'

His fingers were still on her arm, holding her lightly
yet making her intensely aware of the physical contact
between them.

Suddenly there was a glint of amusement in his eyes.
'I'm an Aussie,' he told her. 'The fact that an
Australian woman was one of the prime movers of the
equal rights movement should tell you something about
the Australian male's attitude to women.'

Waiting for him to return, Cassandra was conscious
that the quality of her afternoon ashore had changed.
Her sister was resting in order to be fresh for a party to
which she and Harley had been invited and which might
go on until sunrise. Cassandra had been rather pleased
to come to Lahaina alone and visit the Baldwin House
and the town's public library, neither of which were of
interest to Rosalind.

But now, the chance encounter with Nick Carroll had introduced an element of tension—and, yes, excitement—into her solitary shore excursion. Had she happened to run into any of the other officers she wouldn't have felt like this. None of them had the same effect on her as he did.

He returned with a mug of coffee and a plate with four small cakes on it.

'Chocolate chip cookies,' he said, as he offered them to her.

'Thank you.' She took one. Searching for something to say she caught sight of the name of the bookshop on the bag containing her paperbacks.

'What a strange name—The Upstart Crow and Company. I wonder why the shop is called that?'

'It's a reference to Shakespeare,' he answered. 'One of his fellow playwrights accused him of plagiarism and warned other writers of the day to beware of "an Upstart Crow, beautiful with our feathers". There are quite a lot of Upstart Crow bookshops in America. I've been to branches in San Francisco and San Diego. There's also one in Honolulu.'

Glad to be on safe ground, she said, 'You asked if the books in my cabin weren't the kind I enjoy. The answer to that is that I enjoy almost anything. But I wanted to be able to identify all the flowers I see on my morning walks, and to know how *leis* are made. My sister gave me a lovely carnation *lei* the day I arrived. So I bought these two booklets.'

She opened the paper bag and showed him the contents.

As he flicked through the pages, she added, 'The book I really coveted was the life of Princess Kaiulani. But it was quite expensive and also rather large and heavy and I'm trying to keep my luggage light.'

Nick glanced up. 'That book is by Kristin Zambucka, isn't it?'

She nodded. The unusual name had imprinted itself on her memory. 'You don't know her, do you?'

'No, but she's giving a lecture on Kalakaua, who was Hawaii's last king, at the Lahaina Arts Society tonight. I'm going to hear it. Would you like to come along?'

Cassandra's face glowed. 'I'd love to.'

'She's an artist as well as a writer,' he told her. 'I have a couple of portraits she did years ago, one of a Fijian chief and the other of an Aboriginal girl. Kristin Zambucka is one of the very few white women to have lived with several tribes in the remote Outback.' He rose to his feet. 'I have a couple of things to do before the launch picks us up at half past five. See you later.'

He disappeared down the short escalator which was a somewhat incongruous feature of the Wharf's architecture.

'I'm sorry you can't come to the party, but it's difficult to include you in everything,' said Rosalind, in her sister's cabin about an hour later.

'Of course: I can understand that. Anyway Nick has invited me to go to a lecture with him.'

'How very odd,' said Rosalind thoughtfully. 'It's not like him to be friendly.'

'He was friendly with those two American wives at Pineapple Hill the other night.'

'Yes, with middle-aged frumps and white-haired old ladies he's charming. But I've noticed that it's not only with me he puts on a frosty manner. He's exactly the same with everyone young and attractive. So why is he making an exception of you, I wonder? Perhaps he thinks you're younger than you are. You don't look twenty. You could easily pass for seventeen.'

'That's what he said when he asked me how old I was. Perhaps what you call his frosty manner is something he's learned to adopt towards passengers who might be on the lookout for a shipboard romance. It's probably okay for the other officers to indulge in that sort of thing if they feel inclined, but not for the captain. He has to hold aloof.'

'Aloof is the operative word for Nick Carroll. But inside the Captain's uniform he's still a man, and he must have some kind of sex life. Perhaps he has a Pacific-wide network of women waiting to welcome him in all the places the yacht has been visiting regularly. Although I don't go for those big, brutal, macho types, there are a lot of women who do.'

'He's big, but I don't think you can call him brutal, Ros. I'd say he was quite intellectual.'

Rosalind shrugged. 'All right, maybe not brutal, but certainly macho. Scratch him and under the surface you'll find all the entrenched male attitudes.' She glanced at her Cartier wristwatch. 'I must go and start dressing. What time are you going ashore?'

'At quarter to seven. As we'll miss dinner Nick is arranging for us to have a cold supper later.'

'You'll also miss seeing my new drop-dead gold outfit,' said Rosalind, with a pout.

'You'll be wearing it again, won't you?' asked Cassandra.

'Oh, yes, I shall have to—although there are women who never have to wear the same thing twice. Imagine being able to do that! Maybe some day I will,' her sister said dreamily.

Was that really the summit of Rosalind's ambition? Cassandra wondered, as she waited on the lower deck for Nick to appear.

About half a dozen members of the crew were already seated in the launch. She recognised Olaf, but the others were strangers; men from the galley and the engine room who were normally never seen in the passengers' part of the ship.

Seconds before the appointed time Nick appeared, dressed more casually than for Pineapple Hill in a short-sleeved navy cotton knit shirt and pale khaki cotton pants.

As she sat next to him in the launch, Cassandra felt herself being stared at by the other men in the boat. Was it idle curiosity? Or did everyone know about Ros? Were they wondering if the younger sister was also a girl any man could have if he had enough money?

At the small boat harbour the crew dispersed in the general direction of Front Street, the man in charge of the launch headed back towards *Ocean Wanderer* to be ready when the owner wanted to come ashore, and Nick took her by the elbow and steered her round to the side of the columned Court House on the waterfront side of the banyan tree. Here, steps led down to the basement where bar-enclosed cells indicated that it had been a jail before its conversion to an art gallery.

The audience attending the lecture was very small. Cassandra concluded that either it had not been well publicised or not many people in Maui were interested in the history of Hawaii.

At the end of her talk Miss Zambucka invited questions. Afterwards Nick asked Cassandra to excuse him while he introduced himself as an admirer of the artist's paintings.

Watching him, during the first few moments of his conversation with the gifted New Zealander, she knew she would much rather be having supper with him, and discussing the slide lecture, than going to the party with the others.

The woman sitting next to her made a remark which led to a conversation they continued until Nick returned. Seeing him waiting for them to stop talking, Cassandra took the first opportunity to say, 'I must go now. Good night.'

It wasn't until they were outside that she noticed what he was carrying.

'You've bought one of her books. Which one? The new one, or one of the others?' A number of books by the speaker had been on display.

'I bought two,' he answered. 'The new one for myself and this one for you.' To her astonishment, he handed her the book about Princess Kaiulani which she had been tempted to buy in the Upstart Crow that afternoon.

'I don't know what to say,' she exclaimed. 'It's terribly kind of you, but——'

Before she could find a gracious way to protest that she couldn't accept so extravagant a present, Nick cut in, 'Let's call it an *amende honorable* for being unnecessarily sharp with you on your first night with us. I'm not in the habit of swearing at women. I apologise.'

They were words which, in the first twenty-four hours of their acquaintance, she would never have expected to hear on Nicholas Carroll's lips.

She smiled. 'I deserved that broadside. I should have apologised to you for acting so stupidly. As for this——' she looked down at the book, 'I'm overwhelmed. It's much too generous a gesture, but thank you. Thank you very much.'

'When you've read it, I should like to borrow it, and you can borrow this,' he said, indicating the other book. 'What did you think of the lecture?'

'I was rather amazed so few people turned up.'

'They're probably exhausted from playing golf and sunbathing all day and would rather watch television than make the effort to drive into town,' was his sardonic comment, as they strolled back to the quay. 'But they missed meeting a remarkable woman.'

Cassandra remembered Hugh telling her that the Engineer was a Kiwi. 'Did Mr Hendrickson know about the lecture?' she asked.

'I mentioned it to him, but I knew he wouldn't want to hear it. George has two interests in life—his engines and fishing.'

'Talking of fish, when you told me a local fisherman had trapped some sharks close to shore, were you serious? Or were you exaggerating to impress the dangers on me?'

'Not at all. The *Maui News* had reported that a mackerel fisherman caught three tiger sharks and seven hammerheads a hundred yards off Kauai.'

She remembered how blithely she had been swimming and floating until he had surfaced beside her with the peremptory command to return to the yacht. Had a twelve-foot hammerhead been near . . .

A shudder of horror went through her. 'We might both have been torn to bits!'

'Not necessarily. They say that if you don't panic and wait for a shark to come close, then punch it on the nose, it will usually scare it away,' said Nick. 'But I have to admit I'd prefer not to put it to the test,' he added dryly.

'You may have nerves of steel—I'm sure you have— but I should panic,' said Cassandra. 'How on earth did the fisherman manage to catch all those sharks?'

'He rustled them by their tails and then, one by one, tied on spherical floats. The float stops the shark moving and being able to force fresh seawater through its gills. Without fresh seawater it runs short of oxygen and suffocates.'

'Oh, poor things!'

Her reaction made him laugh. 'You think he should have left them alone?' he asked quizzically. 'That's a bit inconsistent, isn't it?'

'Not really. They belong in the sea. They're part of the balance of nature. We just disport ourselves in it . . . and despoil it with oil leaks and sewage. Why should sharks be annihilated?'

'There's not much danger of that. Atu would tell you a more dangerous fish is a big *onggo*—a barracuda. Inside the reefs, during daylight, you're unlikely to run into either. Don't let them put you off swimming. Far more tourists are injured or drowned by the surf than by accidents with shark or barracuda.'

'Chris says you're an expert surfer. To catch the big waves you have to go outside the reef, don't you?'

'Yes, and very occasionally a surfer goes missing and his board may be found with a chunk bitten out of it. But in general surfing is a lot safer than driving.'

She said, 'You seem to have spent the greater part of your life at sea. How Australian do you feel?'

He considered the question for a moment. 'I suppose, when it comes down to it, the sea is my country. I feel more at home when I step on a deck than I do when I go ashore.'

They had reached the launch. On the short trip out to the yacht, Cassandra held the book on her lap and wondered how she could have thought him an unpleasant man.

It showed how mistaken first impressions could be. Clearly he had received a bad first impression of her but had now revised it. Having got off on the wrong foot with each other, they were now on the right one and, with luck, would stay there.

Atu, who served their supper, had a white plumeria flower stuck in his frizzy black hair. According to Cassandra's book on *leis*, everywhere else the flower was called frangipani, but in Hawaii it was known as plumeria and was used for both single and double *leis*.

'Mr Hendrickson fishes. You surf, read and listen to music. What does Atu do with his spare time?' she asked.

'He takes very little time off. He's always working,' said Nick. 'He and I have been friends since we were children. There's no one I'd rather have with me in a tricky situation. If we ever run into trouble, stick by Atu. He'll take care of you.'

'Are we likely to run into trouble?'

'It's not likely on a vessel of this size, but the Pacific isn't always as friendly as it looks at the moment,' he answered, with a glance at the calm, moon-silvered ocean between Maui and Molokai. 'I remember in 1983 an American girl and her fiancé met an English couple in Tahiti who were tired of cruising and wanted their boat *Hazana* taken to San Diego. The Americans agreed to do it, but they ran into Hurricane Raymond. The girl strapped herself under a table while the man stayed on deck, on a safety line. The boat, a forty-three-footer, rolled completely at least once, knocking her unconscious. When she recovered, she was injured, the boat was badly damaged with both masts broken and the man had been washed overboard. His line was intact, but the harness had snapped.'

Cassandra was listening intently, her food forgotten. As she visualised the grief and terror which the girl must have experienced, a low murmur of pity escaped her.

Nick nodded. 'A terrible situation for anyone, and particularly a girl of twenty-three. But she had a lot of guts and she survived. She rigged up a makeshift sail and used a sextant and her digital watch to navigate. She was alone on *Hazana* for forty-one days before she finally reached Hawaii, the Big Island.'

'Six weeks is a long time to be entirely alone anywhere,' she said. 'But out in the middle of the Pacific ...' She shook her head in wonder at the courage which had got the girl through her ordeal. 'I thought Rosalind and Harley were crossing the Pacific on a boat that size. I was stunned when I saw *Ocean Wanderer*.'

As soon as she had said it, she regretted reminding

him of something which might blight their new rapport.

'I can't see your sister undertaking a long voyage on a small boat,' he said sardonically.

'We both learned to sail a dinghy when we were children. Our aunt had a cottage on the north coast of Norfolk, but the nearest beach was quite a long walk from the village. We used to sail up the estuary when we wanted to picnic on the beach. I loved our holidays there. When the tide was right I spent most of my time in the dinghy.'

'Ever tried windsurfing?'

She shook her head, relieved that they seemed to have skirted the dangerous subject of her sister's relationship with Harley.

'The thing I'd most like to learn is snorkelling,' she told him.

For the rest of the meal the conversation stayed on safe topics and Cassandra was careful to avoid any more unguarded remarks.

When Atu served coffee, Nick invited him to join them. She had the feeling that he was alert to her reaction to this and perhaps, if she hadn't already known they were lifelong friends, she might have been surprised by the Captain inviting the Chief Steward to sit down and chat.

'Has your soul caught up with your body now, Miss Cassandra?' asked Atu, when he was seated opposite her.

As her eyebrows contracted in puzzlement, he gave her his wide, warm smile, and said, 'There's a story about a party of Dutchmen who were exploring West New Guinea long ago. They hired some bearers and set out to climb the Wilhelmina Mountains. The journey wasn't as difficult as they expected and after four days they had travelled a distance they thought would have taken six days. On the fifth morning, coming out of their tents they were surprised to find the bearers still asleep. When they woke them up, the men said, "We can't travel today. We've gone so fast that our souls haven't caught up with our bodies." I think that's what happens to people who fly to the Pacific from America and Europe. But now they call it jet-lag.'

She laughed. 'I know what the bearers meant. I've never felt as peculiar as I did when I landed at Honolulu. I think my soul was still somewhere in the middle of Canada. But it didn't take long to catch up. I felt better the following day.'

'What's the situation with regard to finding someone to help Shaney?' Nick asked Atu.

As Cassandra now knew, the ship's second stewardess had been taken ill a few days before her own arrival and was now in hospital on the island of Oahu recovering from a hysterectomy. Her convalescence would prevent her from rejoining *Ocean Wanderer* during the present voyage and so far no one had been found to replace her.

'No luck, I'm afraid,' Atu answered. 'Shaney and I have interviewed several women today, but nobody suitable. I think we shall have to manage until we reach Fiji. There I can easily find someone.'

'Couldn't I help Mrs Shane?' Cassandra suggested. When they both looked at her in surprise, she went on, 'I'm an experienced housewife. I must have most of the skills a stewardess needs. I'd be glad to give her a hand.'

Atu shook his head. 'No, no—it's kind of you to offer, Miss Cassandra, but you're here to enjoy yourself, not to work.'

'I can do both,' she persisted. 'A few hours' work in the morning will still leave me lots of time for relaxing.'

'Definitely not.' It was Nick who answered her this time and his tone was adamant. 'As Atu says, we appreciate the suggestion, but it wouldn't do. You're

Mr Dennison's guest. He wouldn't like it. You're already doing more than most passengers. Mrs Shane tells me you keep your cabin immaculate.'

'I wouldn't dare not to after the wigging I had on my first night on board!' she answered, daring to tease him.

Then, seeing Atu looking as baffled as she had when he asked her about her soul, she said, 'Haven't you heard about the stupid thing I did that night?' When he shook his head, she continued, 'I went for a swim on my own in the middle of the night. Luckily Nick was about and got me out of the water before anything nasty happened. Telling me to keep my cabin tidy was part of the well-deserved riot act he read me.'

As she spoke, she was slightly nervous that this lighthearted account of the events of that night might strain his friendlier attitude.

But he seemed not to mind it, saying, 'What do you mean about being an experienced housewife?'

'I've spent the past two years keeping house for my father.'

She could see that his next question would be to ask why that had been necessary. To avoid going into details, she said quickly, 'If you'll excuse me, I think I'll go to bed now. Thank you again for taking me to the lecture—and for the book. Good night. Good night, Atu.'

In her cabin she discovered he had asked Kristin Zambucka to autograph the book. As she prepared for bed, she knew that it wasn't only because it was a signed copy of a book she had coveted that she would value it. There was another reason. But she chose to close her mind to that. As soon as she was in bed, she immersed herself in the life story of Princess Kaiulani and continued reading until she couldn't keep her eyes open and was far too sleepy to lie awake thinking about the donor of the biography.

* * *

Early next day, going ashore together, neither of them spoke after exchanging good mornings.

They would talk on the way back to the yacht, and today Nick would ask her to breakfast with him and she would accept, she thought happily.

At the harbour, he gave her his hand to climb out of the launch.

'Thanks. See you.' She started to walk away while he was still shedding his track top.

She had taken only half a dozen paces when the ground shuddered under her feet. What she felt at first was bewilderment. What could be causing such a peculiar sensation? Then she knew what it was. An earth tremor. Perhaps the beginning of an earthquake.

'Nick!' Instinctively she turned to him.

He was only a yard behind her. An instant later she was locked in his arms, her cheek pressed against the warm bare skin of his chest, while under her feet the strange shaking motion continued.

But she was no longer alarmed. It wasn't the unsteady earth which made her blood churn in her veins and her heart beat with rapid thumps. It was being held tightly against him, feeling his strong arms round her and, most of all, knowing that she loved him.

She didn't know how long it lasted. When it stopped neither of them moved.

At length Nick said, over her head, 'I think that was probably Mauna Loa, the volcano over on the Big Island. It certainly wasn't Haleakala here on Maui. If we'd landed a few minutes later, you wouldn't have known it had happened.'

Cassandra stayed very still, not wanting him to release her.

'Are you okay?' He relaxed his hold and felt for her chin, tilting her face up to his.

'I'm f-fine,' she murmured unsteadily.

'If you've never felt one before, a tremor can be pretty scary,' he said, looking down, smiling at her.

'I should have been scared on my own. But not with you,' she answered softly, her heart in her eyes.

She felt him tense and heard his sharp intake of breath. The arm round her tightened again. The fingers under her chin slid round the side of her neck and into the hair at her nape. As his palm and his outspread fingers cupped the back of her head, she knew he was going to kiss her.

It was more than two years since the brother of a school friend had driven her home from a party and kissed her good night. That one half-forgotten experience was no preparation for Nick's experienced embrace.

It was like being caught in the surge of a powerful wave. She felt herself swept by a torrent of strong sensual feelings over which she had no control. Instinctively she resisted, pushing away from his chest, trying to free her mouth from the passionate demand of his warm searching lips.

He let her go almost at once and they confronted each other, both disturbed by what had occurred. He was breathing hard, through his nostrils, the lips which had fused with hers already compressed in a grim line, although the light in his eyes was still hot and desirous.

It was the first time in her life she had been exposed to the almost tangible blaze of a man's desire to possess her.

Part of her quivered with longing to yield to the dynamic force she had felt while she was in his arms and could now see burning in his eyes. Part of her was afraid. She knew she had fallen in love with him. But a week ago she hadn't met him. She wasn't ready for this yet.

The long fraught silence which followed their breaking apart was not unlike another earth tremor.

She felt a tension between them which might ease off or explode.

Nick ended it when he said harshly, 'A sample of what you'll have to put up with if you follow in your sister's footsteps. Perhaps it will make you think twice about taking up her way of life.'

He brushed past her and strode away, soon breaking into a run and disappearing from view.

CHAPTER FOUR

LEFT alone on the quayside, her thoughts and emotions in chaos, Cassandra knew that she needed much more than half an hour's respite before she faced Nick again. She had to get back to the yacht and the privacy of her cabin.

Desperate to avoid another encounter with him until she had pulled herself together, she returned to the launch and, a short time later, was zipping towards *Ocean Wanderer*.

Fortunately several of the deck crew were at work at that hour and one of them saw her come alongside and ran down the ladder to take the mooring line from her.

'Would you find someone to go over and pick up Captain Carroll, please,' she said. 'I had to come back before him.'

In her cabin, she flung herself down on her unmade bed and lay staring with dry-eyed misery at the deckhead, wondering how the moment of joyous certainty she had felt just before Nick kissed her could have turned into a disaster which had put them right back to square one.

She was fairly sure he hadn't meant the contemptuous taunt of his parting shot. It had been the angry reaction of a man who had misunderstood her response to his kiss. She didn't completely understand it herself. She had wanted to be kissed, had enjoyed it—and then, all at once, had panicked when tenderness changed to passion.

But he wasn't to know how little experience she had. Who would imagine that Rosalind's sister, at twenty years old, had never been to bed with anyone?

Another cause of his anger was frustration, she realised. Inexperienced as she was, her intuition told her that it had been quite some time since Nick had held a girl in his arms. As her sister had put it, he was 'as randy as hell', and even Cassandra knew that pent-up sexual desire made a man short-tempered.

But it wasn't as if she had made a deliberate effort to turn him on, and then backed off. At the beginning, their embrace had been spontaneous on both sides. As the ground had shuddered beneath them, they had each reacted in the manner which, in their culture, was conditioned from childhood. He had opened his arms to protect her and she had accepted their shelter, knowing that there was no shield from the forces of nature but nevertheless feeling safer close to his tall, powerful body.

Remembering the scent of his skin, and its smoothness and warmth, she felt herself melting with longing to relive those wonderful moments before the tremor had ended.

They had been, she recognised now, moments of perfect happiness in spite of the turmoil going on beneath the earth's crust. It was a long time since she had been completely happy. There had been degrees of happiness; lilac-scented summer mornings when she had felt glad to be alive; moments of wonder and delight at the magical beauty of a rain-jewelled spider's web, or the angelic voices of the choristers singing carols in King's College chapel.

But total, complete, perfect happiness she had only experienced in the company of someone she loved.

Long ago, when she was little, before she could read well herself, Ros had sometimes read stories to her, the two of them snuggled together on the big shabby sofa in the playroom at the top of the house where they had grown up. That had been happiness.

Later, in Cassandra's teens, after Ros had left home

and before her aunt's death, she and the old lady had sometimes driven along the coast to a beach which in winter always had plenty of driftwood. Warmly wrapped against the bitter North Sea wind, they would gather enough to fill the boot of Miss Vernon's aged black Morris before returning to Vine Cottage for tea and toast by the fire, and long talks about literature and life. That had been happiness.

Since Aunt Esmée's death, life had been mostly loneliness, housework and worries. Even coming to this lovely place of blue skies, sunlight and flowers had been spoiled by the discovery that Ros had become what their aunt would have called, in the idiom of her generation, 'a kept woman'.

Then, last night at the lecture and afterwards, she had had such a comfortable feeling at being on good terms with Nick. She hadn't asked herself why it was a relief no longer to be at loggerheads with him; she had been content that they had begun to be friends and had closed her mind to the possibility of where friendship with such an attractive man might lead her.

Now, after making a hash of it and giving him the impression she hadn't liked it, she couldn't go to him and say, 'Look, please, would you kiss me again, because actually I enjoyed it very much.'

Even if she had the nerve to say that to him, it wouldn't be a good idea. It might be—she had to face it—that what she had felt in his arms wasn't love but infatuation.

Time was what she needed. Time to be sure. But for that damned earth tremor, time was what she would have had. In the ordinary course of events it might have been weeks before he kissed her. If ever.

Later that day Harley's other guests flew in. With a dozen more people on board, suddenly *Ocean Wanderer* seemed crowded with animated Americans.

At dinner that night Cassandra sat between Hugh
Davis and a Californian called Kent who had come to
play golf with Harley and, when they reached Fiji, to
take underwater photographs.

She had some conversation with him before he
became engrossed in talking to his other neighbour.
During the time when Hugh's attention was similarly
engaged, she was left temporarily without anyone to
talk to. It gave her an opportunity to glance at the
other diners, including the Captain.

As he had been at Pineapple Hill, Nick was seated
between two American women, one about his own age
and one in her sixties. Both were extremely vivacious,
chatting almost non-stop to him and to each other,
across him, so that he needed only to interpolate a word
here and there.

When he made a brief smiling comment on
something said by the younger one, whom Cassandra
hadn't yet met, it turned a knife in her heart. Last night
he had smiled at her like that.

At that very moment Nick glanced idly down the
table, his impassive grey gaze passing from face to
face until it reached hers and found her looking at
him.

It was the first look they had exchanged since that
terrible moment ashore when his eyes had been hot with
desire but his voice had been icy with scorn.

Cassandra wanted to look away, but she found she
couldn't. She was transfixed. She could neither blink
nor breathe. Every function seemed to be suspended
except for the beating of her heart and a rush of blood
to her face which spread a deep burning blush from her
cheeks to her forehead and neck.

'Have you heard the latest news about the earth
tremor, Cassandra?' Hugh asked her.

His voice seemed to break the spell. It was a relief to
turn to his kind, pleasant face instead of being forced to

meet the hard, hostile stare fixed on her from the end of the table.

'No . . . no, I haven't,' she answered.

There was no way of disguising the painful flush which had suffused her face. Hugh couldn't fail to see it. But perhaps he hadn't registered what, or rather who, had caused it.

'According to a local news bulletin which I heard while I was changing for dinner, it was the strongest earthquake Hawaii has had for eight years,' he told her. 'There was no damage on Maui, but over on the Big Island there was quite extensive damage. Fortunately the quake hasn't triggered a volcanic eruption. Nor was there any danger of a *tsunami*, a tidal wave. That only happens when the centre is under the sea.'

To keep Hugh talking and give herself time to recover her self-possession, she said, 'There's a volcano on Maui, isn't there?'

'Yes, it's called Haleakala, which means House of the Sun. Going up to see the sun rise over the rim of the crater is one of the island's main tourist attractions—for those who don't mind getting out of bed around four a.m.' He waited until the next course had been served before explaining, 'It's a long drive from here to the summit, but you get some fine views coming down the mountain by daylight. If you'd like to go up, I'd be glad to take you.'

'I'd like to go very much, but if you've been there before, do you really want to see it again?'

'It's several years since I was last up there. I'd like to repeat the experience. After dinner I'll ask around and find out how many of the others are interested. We may need to rent a small tour bus. The problem will be to supply all those who come with warm clothes. At over ten thousand feet it's bitterly cold before sunrise, and most people don't come to Maui with sweaters and gloves in their baggage.'

'That's no problem for me,' said Cassandra. 'I started my journey to Maui dressed for an English cold snap. I can wrap up like an Eskimo.'

'Good. Believe me, you'll need to. In the balmy climate at sea level, people forget what it's like to feel perished. It's no fun waiting for sunrise with chattering teeth and bare legs covered with goosebumps.'

They remained in conversation until the end of the meal. Soon after leaving the table, Cassandra slipped away to her cabin. She felt sure her absence wouldn't be noticed, and she wasn't in the mood to make small talk to a crowd of strangers, however pleasant they might be.

The following day Hugh told her that not many people on board were prepared to be woken at four in order to be on the rim of the crater at sunrise. Apart from themselves, only three others were interested in joining the outing—Chris Knight and two of the new arrivals, Joanne Walters and Bobby Darwin.

'I'm not sure which two they are,' Cassandra confessed, as she and Hugh leaned on the stern rails shortly before lunch was due to be served. 'I expect we've been introduced, but I haven't got everyone sorted out yet.'

He nodded. 'An influx like yesterday's is a bit confusing, isn't it? Joanne was sitting next to the Skipper at dinner last night. Bobby is the lad with the freckles. With only five of us going, we can pack into Mr Dennison's car. He's not using it tomorrow morning and we'll be back before lunch.'

Joanne Walters—who Cassandra took to be the younger of the two women who had sat next to Nick the night before—was in the same place at lunch, although there was someone different on his other side.

Was she there by invitation? Cassandra wondered. She was careful about looking in their direction. Every time she ventured a rapid glance at that end of the table, Nick seemed to be finding Joanne a congenial companion and giving her most of his attention.

It had been arranged that, making as little noise as possible, the volcano party would assemble on the lounge deck for a quick cup of coffee and a hot roll before going ashore.

Cassandra was the first to join Hugh. Then came Chris, followed by Bobby.

'I hope Mrs Walters isn't going to delay us,' said Hugh, with a glance at his watch. 'If she hasn't put in an appearance in five minutes, perhaps you wouldn't mind going to her cabin to see what's happening, Cassandra?'

However, this wasn't necessary. A few moments later Mrs Walters appeared, every shining brunette hair in place and her striking face skilfully made up. Her whole appearance was one of understated elegance. It epitomised the 'look' which Cassandra had decided was the one she wanted to aim for when she and Rosalind had been looking round Brioni.

At the moment she was still a million miles from achieving it. Her own pants were navy needlecords, far from new. Her shirt was pink and grey check worn on top of a cotton spencer. All the garments she had selected for maximum comfort at the top of the volcano were practical, but they weren't co-ordinative and they certainly weren't chic.

This wouldn't have mattered to her if the party had remained at five. But within minutes of Joanne Walters' arrival, Nick appeared.

'You don't mind if I join the expedition, do you, Hugh? Good morning, Joanne. Good morning.'

The second good morning was a cursory acknowledgment of the presence of the rest of the party.

'Not at all, sir. Glad to have you.' However informal they might be with each other in private, Hugh was always punctilious in public.

Perhaps it was out of deference to the younger man's superior rank that, when they were ashore, he asked if Nick wanted to drive.

'No, you drive, Hugh,' was the answer. 'The girls can go in front with you and the rest of us can sit behind.'

'If you don't mind my saying so, I think a better idea is for Cassandra and me to be sandwiched between you four men,' Joanne put in. 'You need to sit in front for the leg room, Nick. If I sit between you and Hugh, the three young people can be together in the back seat.'

Cassandra wondered how he would take having his plan revised, even with the charming smile which Joanne had given him as she made her suggestion.

He didn't seem to mind. 'As you wish.'

Meanwhile the member of the crew who had brought them ashore was loading various containers into the trunk of the car. It was parked not far from where Cassandra had been when the earth tremor started.

She wondered if he had remembered what had happened that morning as they passed the place this morning. She had been intensely aware how on that spot they had stood locked together and, soon after, kissed.

But Nick must have kissed many women. It was years since his first important embrace. If kissing her stayed in his mind, it would be only because she was one or perhaps the only female who had ended an embrace before he was ready to end it.

The first part of the drive to Haleakala was by way of a coast road where the sea rolled in close to the highway.

'If you'd care to use my shoulder as a pillow and go back to sleep for a while, go ahead,' murmured Chris, as the big car sped along the empty road at the edge of the moonlit ocean.

'Thanks, but I'm not sleepy now,' she murmured back.

His offer had caused Nick to turn and glance at the occupants of the back seat. He was sitting with his body turned sideways and his left arm stretched along the back of the bench seat. If Joanne were to lean her head back, her silky, swingy long bob would flow over his forearm.

Cassandra could smell her scent. It pervaded the car, not overpoweringly but like the faint, tantalising aroma of honeysuckle drifting through an open window on a warm summer night.

Hugh said, 'I read in today's *Maui News* that the first humpback whale of the season has been sighted.' He took his eyes off the road for a moment to glance at Joanne. 'A herd which is estimated to be between six hundred and a thousand strong comes to Hawaii every year. They arrive about November and stay until June. They give birth to their calves here. Later in the summer they reappear in Alaskan waters to feed on the huge fields of plankton up there.'

'Shall we see any of them?' she asked, addressing her question to Nick.

'We might be lucky. I doubt it.'

Joanne said, 'When I went shopping in Lahaina yesterday, I was concerned to see how much modern scrimshaw and ivory jewellery is on sale there. I'm sure many people don't realise that when they buy anything new which is made of ivory they're supporting the hunting down of an endangered species.'

Nick said dryly, 'You have no scruples, I notice, about wearing gold jewellery. Doesn't it concern you that a human being had to spend hours underground, in unpleasant conditions, to mine the ore from which your gold was extracted?'

Perhaps it was the first time he had shown his sardonic side to Joanne. Cassandra couldn't see her face, but she sensed that the American woman was startled and momentarily at a loss.

Her recovery was quick. Turning her head to look up at him, she said pleasantly, 'If there were a widespread trend against wearing things made of gold, what other work could the gold miners turn to? Yes, mining is uncivilised. But it's better than starvation.'

Chris gave Cassandra a nudge and, when she glanced at him, winked. Clearly he shared her feeling that in Mrs Walters the Skipper had met his match.

Presently the route to the volcano turned inland across a wide stretch of flat land separating the mountains behind Lahaina from another mountainous area which she took to be the slopes of Haleakala.

As the three in front went on talking, she picked up scraps of information about Joanne's life. Like Hugh, she was divorced. If she received alimony, she supplemented it by working in California as a realtor. This, Cassandra gathered, was the American equivalent of an estate agent. It sounded as if the houses which Joanne sold were in the luxury category. One of her clients had been Harley's cousin Norma, with whom she had become friendly and by whom she had been invited to come on the cruise.

'But I can't stay with you as long as Norma can, unfortunately,' she told the two men. 'Being a working woman I have to get back to my job and hope I'll be able to visit Sydney some other time.'

The remark reminded Cassandra of the problem of her own future which, at the moment, depended on what influence she could bring to bear on her sister. As there wasn't a great deal to see at this stage of the drive, she closed her eyes and leaned her head back against the upholstery, shutting out the others' conversation and concentrating on the difficulties which couldn't be shelved indefinitely.

A light tap on her knee brought her sharply back to an awareness of her surroundings. Before she could open her eyes, she heard Nick say, 'Wake up,

Cassandra!' Then his hand settled on her leg, just above the knee, and shook it.

She sat up with a jerk, waves of sensation spreading up the inside of her thigh from the place where his fingers rested. As she blinked at him, he removed his hand and reached out to shake Chris, rather more roughly.

When Chris had woken up, Nick said, 'That's Kahului over there,' and pointed out the lights of a sizeable town on the edge of the plain they had crossed and which was now spread out below them. 'Give Bobby a nudge, will you, Cassandra?' He replaced his arm on the backrest behind Joanne.

From then on the road ran upwards, at first through a wooded region with houses here and there, and then in a sweeping zig-zag through more open country.

Cassandra was dismayed to find how strong an effect Nick's casual touch had had on her. Just to look at his quarter-profile in the light thrown back from the headlamps made her fingertips tremble with longing to touch that high slanting cheekbone and the angular line of his jaw.

About half a dozen vehicles had arrived at the crater parking lot before them. Once Hugh had switched off the headlamps it was almost pitch dark. Although the sky was bright with stars, there was no moon.

Hugh hadn't exaggerated the cold at that height and that hour of morning. It reminded Cassandra of walking along the towpath in Cambridge in the bleak months after Christmas. She was glad to shrug into her padded anorak and to tie one of her father's foulard silk scarves round her neck before zipping it up.

Her gloves were a pair which had belonged to her aunt.

As she slipped her slim hands inside them, Cassandra felt one of the small pangs which reminders of her aunt often evoked. Perhaps one never stopped missing the people one had once loved—indeed loved still, if only in memory.

Hugh took her arm and lit their path with his flashlight. Nick did the same with Joanne. The two younger men followed behind.

As the sky began slowly to lighten, it could be seen that most of the tourists who had come to see the spectacle were inadequately clad. A few had borrowed the blankets from their hotel beds and were huddling inside them. Several had bare legs and were stamping their feet and apostrophising the sun to hurry up and rise.

Joanne didn't have gloves. After they had been waiting for about ten minutes, and Cassandra's toes were starting to feel cold even inside socks and track shoes, she guessed that Joanne's bare hands must be freezing.

'Why don't you have my gloves?' she offered, pulling them off. 'I have pockets to keep my hands warm. Please, do take them.'

'How very kind of you. Thank you. I almost never wear gloves now that I live on the West Coast. When I do, I invariably lose them. But I shan't take these off until we get back in the car, so I won't lose your gloves,' the American woman said, flexing her fingers inside them.

Cassandra liked her for admitting to being careless. Indeed she liked her so much that she could well understand why Nick, after moving away to speak to Chris for a few moments, soon returned to stand by Joanne.

'I've sent Chris to bring one of the coffee flasks. We have enough with us for a hot drink now and breakfast later, and I think we could all do with something to warm us,' he told her.

'That's a great idea,' she agreed.

'When was the last time this volcano erupted?' asked Joanne, looking up at Nick.

'At the end of the eighteenth century. A few years

RUSH
TIME SENSITIVE

Harlequin Reader Service
2504 W. Southern Avenue
Tempe, Arizona 85282

Postage will be paid by addressee

BUSINESS REPLY CARD
First Class   Permit No. 70   Tempe, AZ

NO POSTAGE
NECESSARY
IF MAILED
IN THE
UNITED STATES

after one of your compatriots, a fur trader called Simon Metcalfe, began what's been called "the fatal impact", meaning the evils introduced by the white man,' he answered. 'Even mosquitoes didn't exist here before then. Now, if they go ashore in the evening without using insect repellent, most people are eaten alive by them.'

'I thought all tropical places had mosquitoes,' said Joanne.

'Maui didn't. Nor did it have any cockroaches, centipedes, scorpions or disease-carrying rats,' he said grimly. 'The mosquito larvae came from ship's water casks; ships which also brought measles and 'flu, both devastating to races who have never been exposed to them.'

'What about leprosy?' asked Joanne. 'Was that indigenous?'

Feeling *de trop*, Cassandra began to edge away. Neither of them seemed to notice.

While she was standing by herself, gazing down into the valley-like crater, Hugh brought her a polystyrene beaker filled with black coffee. He stayed beside her to drink his own coffee. 'I'm afraid I erred on the early side. We could have set out twenty minutes later and had less standing about.'

'It doesn't matter, Hugh. We're all well muffled up. I feel sorry for some of the others.'

Cassandra noticed that Nick had produced a hip flask and was lacing Joanne's coffee with brandy or possibly rum. She was smiling up at him. Before he added a generous dash of the spirit to his own beaker, he gave her the attractive grin he usually reserved for older women.

They were ideally matched, thought Cassandra, with a sinking feeling. Two of a kind. Clearly Joanne was a match for him in more ways than holding her own with him in conversation. It was a pity she had a failed marriage behind her, but perhaps the one most at fault had been her ex-husband.

'. . . won't be long now,' remarked Hugh, breaking into her reverie.

With a guilty start, she realised she had completely switched off and poor Hugh had been talking to himself, except for the last few words.

As she could see that he knew this, she hastened to apologise.

'I'm so sorry, Hugh. For a minute or two I was miles away.'

He looked at her kindly. 'If this is your first long trip, I expect you sometimes feel homesick. I know I did on my first voyage. It was an exciting time, but there were moments, I remember, when I felt a long way away from——

He broke off and they both remained silent as the edge of a great red-gold orb began to emerge, as if from the depths of the pale, pearl-coloured ocean they could see beyond and below the far rim of the crater.

A hush fell over the people—fifty or sixty of them now—who, from all parts of the island, had converged on the look-out to see the sun take possession of the eerie dead-planet world within the crater.

For the next few minutes all eyes would be fixed on the fiery ball of distant heat as it came fully into view; or so Cassandra thought, as she turned her own gaze towards Nick and Joanne.

As she expected, Joanne was intently watching the sunrise, but it was a disconcerting surprise to find that Nick wasn't. He was looking directly at Cassandra, with an expression of annoyance, not to say anger, on his face.

She looked away, startled and hurt by that glare of black disapproval. Was her mere presence among them an irritation? Was he furious with himself because, for one evening, he had softened towards her and, the next day, allowed his sex hunger to overrule his better judgment?

It was some time before the sun had risen high enough to penetrate the crater, and by then many of the watchers were too chilled to want to linger until it reached the crater floor, several thousand feet below the rim. They began to disperse.

'I think we might move on up to the Observatory, Hugh,' said Nick, coming up behind them.

His expression was no longer angry, but, even addressing his second-in-command, he spoke with a certain curtness.

'A good idea,' agreed Hugh, turning away.

Cassandra would have followed him, but Nick said, 'Let me get rid of that for you,' and took the empty polystyrene beaker from her hand.

'Thank you.'

As he tossed it, with his, into a litter container, she noticed Joanne had fallen into conversation with the elderly Americans whom he had helped earlier on.

'I thought you had gloves,' he remarked, as Cassandra blew on her bare hands.

'I lent them to Mrs Walters. She has no pockets,' she said stiffly.

'Give your hands to me.'

To her amazement, he seized them and began to massage them. At first she was too dumbfounded to react. For perhaps half a minute she submitted to having the warmth restored to her fingers by the strong stroking movements of his. Then the feel of his thumbs circling her palms became too much to bear.

She snatched her hands free and said hoarsely, 'They're fine now.' She thrust them back into her pockets.

It was almost a repetition of what had happened on the quayside a few days before. They stood, less than an arm's length apart, Cassandra's height dwarfed by his, her firm chin lifted defensively.

But this time it wasn't desire that burned in Nick's slate-grey eyes. It was anger; a wrathful glint in which she could read, all too plainly, his impulse to shake her.

She removed the temptation by uttering another cold, 'Thank you,' and walking away.

A couple of hours later, after stopping on the way down to look at the strange and rare silversword plants which were peculiar to the highlands of Maui and Hawaii, they had a picnic breakfast in a meadow sheltered by a grove of tall eucalyptus trees.

Joanne had been told that the uplands of Maui were where many of the proteas bought by flower arrangers in the United States were grown.

'I'd like to buy some. Have we time?' she asked Nick.

It was Cassandra's impression that the four men had been rather bored by the visit to the protea gardens. She was surprised when, on returning to the car, Joanne had another request. She had heard of a shop in a place called Paia which sold early examples of aloha shirts. She wanted to see what they were like and perhaps buy one as a souvenir.

Talking about this, later in the day, to her sister, Cassandra said, 'Joanne kept them hanging about in Paia for almost an hour while she and I looked round the dress shops. It didn't seem to worry her that they had nothing to do there.'

'It wouldn't. American women don't have the same hang-ups we have. In Europe we're brought up to believe that it's okay for us to be bored out of our minds watching rugger or cricket or whatever, or listening to interminable discussions about cars and politics and investments, but we must never expect men to sit through a fashion show or listen to feminine chit-chat.'

'That was true of Father's generation, but is it still?' Cassandra said doubtfully. 'A lot of women are interested in politics and, if I had any money, I'd be interested in investments.'

'Okay, so there's more overlapping of interests than there used to be,' Rosalind conceded. 'But if what I'm saying isn't true, why did you feel worried about keeping them waiting this morning? I don't suppose they minded propping up a bar for an hour. I'll bet Nick didn't. Any boredom he suffered will be more than offset by the undivided attention he gets from Joanne in her cabin,' she added, with a laugh.

Cassandra tensed. 'What do you mean?'

'Don't be naïve! I could see what was going to happen the moment she came on board. And why not?' said Rosalind, shrugging. 'Perhaps sleeping with her will make him less supercilious.'

When everyone assembled on the lounge deck for drinks before dinner Joanne was looking cool and elegant in a long sleeveless shift of black cotton with an Indian silver necklace. Long slits in the side seams showed her legs when she moved.

Harley had had his fill of playing golf at Kapalua and was ready to embark for the eastern end of the island.

'We'll be leaving our present anchorage after breakfast,' he announced to his guests. 'Hugh wants to make the road trip. He can take five passengers if any of you want to join him. But I hear it's a long, winding drive, so I'd recommend you to stay on board and see the coastline in comfort.'

Joanne didn't sit next to Nick at dinner that night. Nor did Cassandra see her talking to him before the meal or afterwards. But if they were spending their nights together, they could afford to be discreet in public, she thought unhappily.

She could understand Nick being attracted to the American woman. Cassandra herself admired Joanne and hoped that, when she reached her thirties, she could be as poised and together as Joanne was.

If Ros were right about them, it suggested a ship-board fling rather than the beginning of a long-term relationship, and it diminished her respect for them. It put Nick on a par with Terry Anson who might have a preference for Ros but who, in Cassandra's opinion, would quickly find his way to the cabin of any female on the yacht who signalled that he would be welcome.

Before going below that night, she asked Hugh how many people were going with him the next day.

'Nobody. Why? Would you like to come?' he asked.

'Would you mind?'

'I'd be glad of your company.'

It was late afternoon when they reached the small, quiet town of Hana.

From the moment of setting out, Cassandra had made a strong effort not to allow her personal problems to cloud her enjoyment of the drive.

Perhaps it was partly because she had done little travelling that she found the journey enthralling. The road *was* a series of bends. The surface *was* rough in places. But for her, as a passenger, free to sit back and look about, it was also a succession of visual delights as the road meandered in and out of steep, thickly forested gullies, many with streams and waterfalls cascading down them.

Had they driven without stopping, it would have taken less than three hours. But they stopped many times on the way for Hugh to take photographs at outstanding beauty spots, and also to share a packed lunch at one of the many lovely picnic places.

When their route into Hana reached a crossroads, Hugh turned left down a short hill which brought them to a beach with a concrete jetty at the far end of it. *Ocean Wanderer* had arrived before them. She was moored in the bay. As they left the car they saw the launch heading shorewards, full of passengers.

After a brief conversation with the party coming ashore for a stroll round the town, she and Hugh took their place in the launch, both of them looking forward to cooling off in the shower.

Long before they came alongside, she had recognised the tall figure standing at the top of the boarding ladder. The sight of him instantly revived all the troublesome thoughts she had determinedly ignored during the drive.

'We were beginning to think you'd had a breakdown,' said Nick, when they joined him on deck.

'We took our time. There's a lot to see. It was an interesting drive, wasn't it, Cassie?'

It was the second time he had abbreviated her name. If it had to be shortened she preferred the form Rosalind used, but she hadn't told him that.

'Yes, it was great,' she agreed.

'See you later.' Hugh put a hand on her shoulder and gave it a friendly squeeze.

As he moved off, she said, 'I need a shower. Excuse me.'

'When you've cleaned up, I'd like a word with you . . . in private.' Nick looked at his watch. 'Come to my quarters in half an hour, would you, please?'

Although politely phrased, it was unmistakably an order. Wondering what on earth he could want with her, Cassandra murmured assent and walked away.

It was unlikely that Nick had commanded her presence in his private quarters in order to be sociable. What had happened after the earth tremor had made it impossible for them ever to be on the relaxed, comfortable terms she enjoyed with Hugh.

As she didn't know where his quarters were, she had to ask Josaia, one of the stewards, to show her. When they arrived at a door marked *Captain*, he tapped on it.

From inside came a brisk instruction to enter.

Josaia opened the door for her, his smile bolstering her morale as she thanked him and stepped inside Nick's domain.

A desk with a swivel chair, a small filing cabinet, two linen-covered armchairs and a coffee table were the only furnishings. The cabin was part sitting-room, part office, but it gave an immediate impression that its occupant was a man of cultivated tastes, an impression reinforced by the fact that when Josaia knocked Nick had been sitting listening to a piece of classical music which she didn't recognise.

He had risen to his feet as the door opened. Now he said, 'Sit down, Cassandra,' and moved to switch off the music. 'What can I give you to drink?'

This was unexpected. She had thought he would come to the point of the interview without any social preliminaries.

Before she could answer, he went on, 'Pineapple juice is your usual aperitif, isn't it?' and opened a small refrigerator stocked with tall cartons of fruit juice, cans of beer, an opened bottle of white wine and an unopened bottle of champagne.

It surprised her that he'd noticed what she usually drank before dinner when the others were having Mai Tais, rum punches and Blue Hawaiians.

'Or perhaps you'd rather join me in a gin and tonic?' His manner was smooth, affable—and, she was certain, assumed.

'Yes, thank you, I will,' she replied, reminding herself that she was a woman of twenty, even if not a very sophisticated one, and only subject to Nick's jurisdiction in matters to do with the running of the ship and the safety of the people on board.

In everything else Harley was the final arbiter.

'I've been meaning to ask you what you meant by claiming to be an experienced housewife,' he asked, as he fixed a drink for her.

'It wasn't a claim. It was a statement of fact. Between leaving school and coming out here, I was my father's housekeeper.'

Nick handed her a tall glass with ice cubes and a slice from a fresh lime floating near the brim.

'Why was that?' he asked, sitting down.

She said, in a matter-of-fact tone, 'He was ill. There was no one else who could give him the care he needed. It's amazing how well some stroke patients can recover if they receive the right help and aren't just left to vegetate. But it doesn't always work. It didn't in my father's case.'

He gave her a long thoughtful look. 'It must have been a very hard time for you. Eighteen is too young to be saddled with that kind of responsibility. Did your sister know your father was ill?'

She avoided his eyes. 'No, she didn't.'

It wasn't the truth. Ros had known. But Cassandra wasn't going to give him another reason to dislike her sister, or to go into the reasons why Rosalind's return had been out of the question. Suddenly she thought she saw the reason why he wanted to talk to her.

'Have you changed your mind about refusing my offer to help Mrs Shane?'

'No, that problem is solved—or it will be as soon as we reach Fiji. She can manage until then.'

He swirled the ice in his glass, making her notice, not for the first time, the length of his lean, square-tipped fingers and the strength of his wrists. She remembered how it had felt when those fingers had brushed her neck and cradled her head, holding it in place for his kiss. She remembered the hardness of his arm enclosing her and the softness of his mouth moving on hers. She felt a sharp longing to repeat the experience. But she knew it would never happen again. Even if he hadn't been involved with Joanne now, she had done an unforgivable thing —repulsed him. From what she had read, there wasn't a male ego in the world which could forgive or forget that.

She said, 'Why then? I mean, why did you want to see me?'

He said, with an edge of sarcasm, 'You'd prefer to be on deck, I take it?' With a single lithe movement, he rose. 'Don't worry, I shan't keep you long. You can finish your drink with the others. I asked you to come here to advise you to spend less time with Hugh.'

Her eyes widened in astonishment. 'Why?' she asked blankly.

Nick thrust his hands into the pockets of his shorts. She could see the outlines of his clenched knuckles through the white cotton.

He said, 'Hugh was devoted to his wife. Although they were separated for long periods, he never looked at another woman. It was a tremendous blow to learn recently that she had found someone else. He's lonely and vulnerable. I don't want to see him hurt again—which could happen if you continue to spend most of your time with him.'

It was such an unfair indictment that Cassandra was outraged. She said angrily, 'You can hardly blame me for the fact that nobody else was interested in seeing the road to Hana today. Was I supposed to miss an interesting experience because the others preferred to spend the day lazing on deck?'

'No, but it might be prudent to avoid any more excursions *à deux*.'

'That suggestion is demeaning to both of us—to Hugh and to me,' she retorted. 'I'm sure it's never entered his head to regard me as anything but . . . but a young girl who's rather out of her element in this sort of milieu. From my point of view he's a kind, sympathetic older friend. He's the only person on board who I'm really comfortable with. I have no intention of suddenly starting to avoid him.'

'I didn't suggest that you should; merely that it would

be better to spend more time with other people, including the members of your own sex,' he added dryly.

The implication in this remark made Cassandra even more furious. She said hotly, 'Just because you——'

As she bit off the end of the statement she was thinking of him and Joanne falling into bed together within a few days of meeting.

His face was as hard as it had been the first time they met.

'Go on: don't be afraid to speak your mind. Because I . . . what?'

She took a deep breath. 'Just because you can't control your sexual urges, it doesn't mean everybody can't.'

As she said it, a wave of hot colour swept over her face. She wasn't used to talking about sex to a man. Her father had never mentioned the subject. When she was nine or ten Aunt Esmée had explained her reproductive system to her. And she and her three closest school friends had theorised a good deal. None of them had had much practical experience before leaving school. They had all been bright girls, potential achievers, members of a generation who were starting to re-think and amend the permissive code which had been in force for some time.

Maybe by now the other three had had lovers. Or maybe not. They weren't the kind of girls to do anything because of peer pressure. But whatever had happened to them, her own life had been as cloistered as that of a novice. Until Nick had kissed her. But it hadn't made her more at ease with him.

His dark grey eyes narrowed. 'If you can't handle being kissed by me, you're not going to find it any easier to deal with Hugh when he disproves your theory that he sees you just as a friend.'

'He won't.' She leaned forward to put her glass on the coffee table. Then she stood up. 'May I go now . . . Captain?'

The grinding of his teeth was betrayed by the sudden bunching of muscle at the angle of his jaw. But his voice remained low and controlled as he said, 'No, you may not. I haven't finished with you yet.'

The punitive glint in his eyes made her quail, but she lifted her chin and said coldly, 'If you don't approve of my behaviour, why not complain to Mr Dennison?'

As soon as she'd said it, she regretted it. Putting herself under Harley's wing when she deplored her sister's place in his life was an unworthy defensive strategy.

She could see by the curl of Nick's lip that he thought the same. She wished she could retract the suggestion.

Nick moved from where he was standing and came to within a yard of her. His hands were still out of sight, but she had the feeling that, if she tried to turn tail, they would flash from his pockets as fast as the action of one of those predatory lizards with a long whip-like tongue which flicked out to snap up unwary insects.

'Tell me something,' he said, in a dangerously bland tone. 'When you clung to me at the harbour a few days ago, was it only because you were frightened? Or were you willing to be kissed—up to a point?'

Her face began to burn again. Why had he brought up that incident? Was he going to take her reply and, like a clever attorney, twist it round and use it against her?

What could she answer? Not the truth. *Yes, I wanted to be kissed. I'd just discovered I loved you. But it was virtually my first kiss and I felt myself being swept away by someone I hardly knew. It was too soon ... too overwhelming ...*

Nick moved a short pace closer, making her edge back. Suddenly the cabin seemed tiny: a small claustrophobic space in which she was trapped with this tall unpredictable man, still as much of a stranger as he had been that morning on the quay. But a stranger who, if he chose, could put her emotions in tumult.

She backed into the door and, startled, gave a slight gasp. Unless she whirled round and scrabbled ignominiously to open it—and she knew he wouldn't allow her to escape without answering his question—her retreat was over.

'You don't want to answer that, do you? I'll tell you what I think, shall I?'

He jerked his hands out of his pockets and slapped them against the door panel on either side of her head. He leaned his weight on his arms; bringing his torso so close she could smell the fresh clean aroma of his soap or shampoo.

Looking down at her, he said softly, 'I think you enjoy playing with matches but if, when you've set things alight, it looks like becoming a bush fire, you don't want to know. Things got a little hotter than you intended that morning and you got panicky—right? I don't know why. We were in a public place. You weren't in much danger of having to be as generous with your favours as your sister is with hers.'

Cassandra's eyes flashed with anger. 'That's the second time you've insulted my sister! You wouldn't dare to refer to her in those terms in Harley's hearing,' she flared at him. 'You know nothing about Rosalind— except that she and Mr Dennison aren't married. You don't seem to have a low opinion of Joanne. But that's different, I suppose. She's sleeping with *you*.'

There was an electric moment when the tension between them was such that she held her breath.

It was a surprise when, instead of exploding with wrath, he said quietly, 'What gave you that idea?' And then, with unnerving shrewdness, 'Or should I say who?'

Fortunately he didn't wait for her answer, but went on, 'Whoever it was, they were spreading unfounded gossip ... slanderous gossip. I can't vouch for the passengers' conduct, among themselves, but the officers and crew of this ship only mix with them during daylight and within certain limits.'

'Which you chose to ignore the other morning.'

'Kissing a girl who invites it isn't proscribed,' he said dryly.

'That's not true. I didn't invite it. I admit I was glad to be close to you during the tremor, but I didn't invite you to kiss me.'

'Not in so many words. But you nestled against me. You didn't look cross, as you do now.' He lowered his head a fraction, causing her heart to lurch wildly. 'You smiled at me, if you remember. I can read a clear signal to go ahead when I see it.'

Of course it *was* true. But if she couldn't dispute it, she wasn't going to admit it. She took refuge in silence and an expressionless gaze fixed on the topmost button of his open-necked shirt. The next move was up to him. When she thought what it might be, a frisson ran down her spine and her insides clenched with suspense.

Close to him like this, trapped between him and the door, she forgot everything but the dizzying physical magnetism which he exerted upon her.

It seemed a long time that they stayed as they were, neither speaking. Slowly, against her will, Cassandra found herself raising her eyes from the shirt button up to his brown throat and then higher, up to his face.

It was hard to interpret the look that met hers. What was he waiting for? she wondered. If he was going to kiss her again, why didn't he get on with it?

But still the taut silence continued while he bent that oddly stern gaze on her uplifted face.

From the other side of the cabin, a chirping sound started. Nick muttered something pithy under his breath. He straightened and turned away, leaving Cassandra torn between relief and disappointment.

She watched him depress a button on an intercom system and say curtly, 'Yes?'

Although she could hear the voice of whoever was calling him, the man was speaking a language she couldn't understand.

Nick answered in the same language. After a brief exchange, he concluded the call and said to her, 'I'm afraid you'll have to excuse me, but stay and finish your drink.' A gleam of mockery lit his eyes. 'I'm sure you could do with it.'

A moment later he had gone, closing the door behind him and leaving her alone.

Not knowing how long he would be absent, and having no wish to be found there when he returned—which he would undoubtedly take as further evidence of her liking for playing with fire—she picked up the drink he had given her and swallowed some of the weak gin and tonic.

Allowing herself a few minutes to look at the titles crowding the bookshelves and the paintings and drawings which hung almost edge to edge on the opposite bulkhead, she wondered if Nick had been speaking the truth when he had denied any intimate relationship between himself and Joanne Walters.

She didn't think he was a liar. Nor was she. But sometimes normally truthful people did tell lies to protect other people. Could she believe him about Joanne? And, if it were true that they weren't on those terms, didn't it perhaps suggest that something more serious than a shipboard affair might be brewing between them?

What, if Joanne meant nothing to him, had made him refrain from kissing Cassandra a few minutes ago? It had been in his mind, she was certain. But for some reason he had hesitated to act on the impulse. Why?

As she looked around her, seeking fresh clues to the personality of the man who had suddenly become the most important person in her life, there was a knock at the door.

Because her nerves were still on edge from the stressful scene with Nick, the sound made her jump. For a few seconds, as if she were in a place where she had no right to be, she froze.

As she stood there, staring uncertainly at the door, wondering who was outside, she realised it hadn't been a brisk loud rap such as one of the stewards or the deck crew would give. It had been a light rapid tap—the sound of feminine knuckles.

CHAPTER FIVE

THE door opened. Instead of the elegant woman Cassandra had expected to see, Mrs Shane's shorter, plumper figure came into view.

The stewardess stopped short, obviously startled at finding someone in the cabin.

'Oh . . . you gave me a start, Miss Cassandra. I'm just bringing back these two shirts. Is the Captain through there'—with a nod towards the inner cabin.

'No, he was called away. I'm just finishing my drink,' Cassandra explained.

She wondered if Mrs Shane would show surprise that her beloved Captain Nick should invite the least important passenger to have a private pre-dinner drink with him.

But the little Australian woman seemed to see nothing odd in it, or was too well trained to reveal her reactions. She said, 'The stewards look after the other gentlemen's laundry, but these good shirts he wears ashore I prefer to wash out by hand. They last twice as long. He can't afford to have his clothes racked and ruined, not while he's saving for his schooner.'

'His schooner?' Cassandra repeated.

'That's what he wants and, knowing him, that's what he'll have. A schooner and a nice wife to make him as happy as Captain Ted was with his mother; those are the two things Captain Nick has set his heart on.'

'Really? I had the impression the Captain probably preferred to remain a bachelor.'

At this Mrs Shane did show surprise. 'Oh, no, dear—no, not at all. I won't say he didn't have his fling when he was younger. What good-looking bloke in his twenties doesn't? But the Captain of a ship can't afford to have a bad reputation with women—not like some I could mention,' she added, clicking her tongue. 'Anyway Captain Nick isn't a ladies' man by nature. He's been looking for a wife for a long time. But it isn't easy to find someone who'll be right for the life he wants. He could never be happy ashore. A couple of weeks in Sydney and he starts getting restless. A wife with a hankering for terra firma would never make him happy.'

By this time she had bustled through to the inner cabin and was putting the shirts in a sliding tray in the closet while Cassandra stood on the threshold, looking round with even greater curiosity at Nick's inner sanctum.

'Very neat and tidy, the Captain is,' said Mrs Shane. 'Most sea-faring men are, you'll find. That's another thing he couldn't stand—an untidy wife. You're very neat, Miss Cassandra, and so is Mrs Walters.' She closed the door of the closet. 'You and your sister must have had the same upbringing, but you couldn't be more different, could you?'

'No, we aren't much alike,' Cassandra agreed. 'I don't remember my mother but Rosalind is said to take after her. I'm more like my father's sister.'

'It's funny where likenesses come from,' said the stewardess. 'Captain Nick does resemble his father.' She beckoned Cassandra to come further inside the cabin. Her reason for this was that hanging on the part of the wood-panelled bulkhead hidden by the open door was a framed collage of photographs, some studio portraits, some snapshots.

'That's Captain Ted and his bride on their wedding day,' said Mrs Shane. 'When you can't see his features closely, it could be Captain Nick, couldn't it?'

Cassandra nodded. It brought a lump to her throat to look at the bridal couple; the tall, deeply tanned man

in a white naval-style uniform looking so much like
Nick as he smiled at the slender girl on his arm, her
white veil blowing in a breeze.

The late Mrs Carroll had indeed been a ravishing girl,
and with something vaguely familiar about her face
which Cassandra couldn't pin down.

'That's the Captain with Atu, the Chief Steward,
when they were boys.' Mrs Shane's finger had moved to
a snapshot of a pair of ten year old boys, both wearing
colourful Fijian *sulus*, posed with an arm round each
other's shoulders.

'Who's that?' Cassandra asked, noticing a photograph
of a laughing girl with black hair combed straight out
from her scalp and neatly trimmed into a ball-shape.

'That's Eleni, a Fijian girl. Her grandfather was
friendly with Captain Ted. Of all the people in the
Pacific, the Fijians were the ones he liked best. He
received a lot of kindness from them, and when Eleni
went to Australia to train to be a teacher, Captain Nick
made sure she was looked after by his relations in
Sydney.'

When they returned to the day cabin she pointed out
one of the paintings. It had caught Cassandra's eye
earlier; a watercolour of a graceful sailing vessel
moored alongside a busy wharf somewhere in the
Pacific.

'There—that's what his heart is set on,' said the
stewardess. 'And I have an idea it won't be long before
he has his own ship and a wife.' She gave Cassandra a
conspiratorial glance. 'It's my belief this cruise will end
with a wedding.' She paused, her expression expectant.
When no comment from Cassandra was forthcoming,
she glanced at the clock on Nick's desk, and said, 'But I
musn't keep you chatting. They'll be serving dinner
shortly.'

Cassandra would have liked to skip dinner that night.
But she knew she couldn't. It was with a heavy heart

that she made her way up to the lounge deck. She doubted that, as his former nanny, Mrs Shane was privy to all Nick's amours. He had probably had some relationships of which she knew nothing. But as a close observer of his lifestyle for the past three years, and with a knowledge of his character built up over many years' connection with his family, she was in a position to do some intelligent guesswork about his marital intentions. Clearly she had been sounding out Cassandra in the hope of having her conjectures confirmed by someone who saw Nick and Joanne together more often than she did herself.

Arriving on deck, almost the first person Cassandra saw was Joanne, wearing her black linen shift with a different but equally striking necklace of vivid blue turquoise beads. Unlike Rosalind who rarely appeared in the same garment twice, the American seemed to have a small basic wardrobe but a lot of unusual jewellery and accessories.

Catching sight of Cassandra, she came over to her, and asked, 'How was the drive? Did you enjoy it?'

Cassandra had temporarily forgotten the reason why Nick had summoned her to his cabin and his homily about her relationship with Hugh. What had followed had driven it from her mind.

'Yes, you missed an interesting experience.'

Suddenly she knew why it was Nick's mother's face had seemed vaguely familiar. Mrs Carroll had had curly hair and had worn little or no make-up when the photograph was taken, but she had borne a marked resemblance to Joanne Walters.

If anything were needed to confirm Mrs Shane's supposition, this was it. The first woman a man loved was his mother. Joanne's physical resemblance must have sparked an immediate interest which, presumably, had strengthened with closer acquaintance.

'Yes, I'm sure I did,' Joanne agreed, in reply to

Cassandra's remark. 'I did consider coming with you but then I decided to be lazy. The last month or two I've been working very hard and I need to unwind and relax.'

And to stay where Nick is, rather that going on expeditions which his duties prevent him from joining, thought Cassandra.

She said, 'What a stunning necklace.'

'Thank you. I bought it in Mexico which is a great place to shop. I wonder what Fiji will be like for shopping? Not that I'll be there long. I have to go back immediately after Christmas. Norma has been trying to persuade me to give up my job and stay with the cruise to Sydney. Then she wants me to spend a couple of months touring Australia with her. It's a tempting suggestion, but I don't know that I dare risk letting my present job go.'

At this point they were joined by Harley's cousin Norma. Shortly afterwards Atu announced dinner whereupon Norma swept Joanne away and a few moments later Cassandra saw them taking the places on either side of Nick.

Clearly, like Mrs Shane, Norma had seen which way the wind was blowing and was eager to promote a romance between her protégée and the personable Australian. Perhaps neither she nor Joanne was as yet aware that Nick's future wife wouldn't be living in luxury on board *Ocean Wanderer* but on a much smaller vessel.

Cassandra admired Joanne. As well as being attractive and chic, she was outgoing, well-read and sensible. Except for having one failed marriage behind her, she had no obvious flaws and many likeable qualities. But she did strike the younger girl as being very much an urban person who might not easily adapt to the life which he had in mind.

*　　*

Heavenly Hana, as the small town was called, was indeed an idyllic retreat from the world in which most people were obliged to live.

That afternoon all the passengers and some of the officers and crew went swimming at Hamoa Beach, a crescent of sand, shaded by pandanus trees, a little way south of the town.

By this time Cassandra had lost her pallor and was a pale golden brown all over except for the areas covered by her bikini. She was still carefully using a high protection factor sun-cream on every inch of exposed skin, including her lips and eyelids.

Joanne didn't expose her face to the sun at all. She applied a total sun-block and also wore a wide-brimmed hat of vivid emerald straw which she had bought in Lahaina.

Most of the men were in the water, but the big waves surging towards the beach were deterring most of the women from joining them. Harley, as usual, was golfing. Ros was strolling along the beach with Terry Anson. Like many red-haired people he was always in danger of blistering and never stayed in the sun for long without a tee-shirt.

It must be an annoying disadvantage, thought Cassandra, with a twinkle in her eyes, for a dedicated Don Juan to be cursed with a nose which had to be slathered with a special white cream to prevent it burning, and with arms and legs which tended to redden rather than brown. Not that Terry let it cramp his style, was her next, less amused thought. The other women were beginning to exchange glances when, in Harley's absence, he flirted with her sister. That they didn't like Ros was obvious. She encouraged their antipathy by all but ignoring them.

Since she had stopped going ashore with Nick, Cassandra had felt under-exercised. She took off her watch, which wasn't waterproof, and walked down to the water's edge. She had never swum in a sea with strong surf rolling in and inwardly she was a bit nervous. But she felt she had to try it. This surf wasn't like the enormous, terrifying surf of the Banzai Pipeline, and there were plenty of people to come to her aid if she yelled for help.

The warm foam was swirling round her knees when Atu came out of the water, his dark skin glistening, his short thick black hair silvered with droplets.

'You're not afraid of getting wet, eh, Miss Cassandra?' he said, directing a rather disdainful glance at the other women reclining under the sunbrellas the crew had put up for them.

'Not of getting wet—no. But I have a healthy respect for these breakers. I'm not as strong a swimmer as you are, Atu.'

'You'll be okay. Dive into the waves before they have a chance to knock you over. I'll stay close to you, if you like.'

'I wish you would, just at first,' she said gratefully. Like Nick, Atu was a man in whom, in any emergency, she would have total confidence.

They hadn't been in the water long when Nick joined them.

'Aren't any of the other women coming in?' he asked her.

He was really only interested in Joanne, she guessed.

'I don't know. It is a bit rough.'

'You seem to be enjoying yourself.'

'Atu has been lifeguarding me.'

But Atu had gone, she discovered. Already he was some yards away, joining in boisterous horseplay with the other stewards, all of them shouting with laughter. Watching their schoolboyish game, her own face breaking into a grin at the fun they were having, Cassandra forgot to keep an eye on the breakers.

Nick had already duck-dived, but the wave had

caught her in its rolling action when she tried to avoid it. She found herself flung about like a mouse in a washing machine, without a full intake of air to last her through the long moments while it tumbled her over.

When she surfaced, she was gasping for breath and her hair was all over her face, clinging like seaweed, blinding her. As she trod water and struggled to remove the sticky strands, strong hands came from behind her and grasped her under the arms. She felt herself being drawn backwards and, knowing who it was, relaxed and let him support her while she used both sets of fingers to comb back her tangled hair.

It must have been one of the lulls which came between sets of big breakers. There were no more large combers while he towed her into shallow water.

For a moment or two, before her feet touched bottom, her back was against his chest. As his hands slid down from her armpits to her waist, the tips of his fingers brushed the sides of her breasts where they weren't covered by her bikini top. It was, she felt sure, an unintentional contact, and of the most fleeting duration, but, light and brief as it was, it gave her a shock of pleasure to feel him touching her there.

Nick held her by the waist until he could tell her feet were planted on the sand and she was braced to stay upright in the vigorous push and pull of the, for her, chest-deep water.

'Thank you,' she said breathlessly, turning to him.

'Surf sneaks up on you, if you don't watch it. Doesn't matter much here, but it can mean some nasty grazes if there's coral about. Coral cuts take a long time to heal. It's best to avoid them,' he told her.

As he swung away and waded on to the beach, Cassandra watched the ripple of muscle under the wet brown skin of his wedge-shaped back and found herself wondering what she would have done if, under the water, he had slipped his hands further round to cover her breasts and hold them.

Of course he would never do that. Terry Anson was the type to go in for furtive caresses, but Nick wasn't. Anyway, he obviously preferred a figure like Joanne's. Although she had long slim legs, her breasts and hips were more generously curved than Cassandra's. Today they were displayed to advantage in a plain black strapless one-piece with a satin finish which emphasised her shapely contours as she moved about taking photographs of the other women and the beach.

'Shall I take one of you?' Cassandra heard Nick ask her.

'Would you, please?' Then Joanne noticed Cassandra coming up the beach behind him and had a better idea. 'Cassandra, would you take a picture of Nick and me, please?' She gave him a ravishing smile from under the brim of her green hat. 'I must have one of *Ocean Wanderer*'s Captain for my album.

They looked perfect together; a well-matched pair in height, age, good looks and style. Captain and Mrs Nicholas Carroll. As she peered at them through the view-finder what Cassandra saw in her mind's eye was the picture of Nick's father's wedding, but with Nick and Joanne in place of Captain Ted and his bride.

'The next one's the last on the roll,' said Joanne, as she took back the camera. 'Why don't I take a picture of the two of you for Cassandra's album?'

'Cassandra may not want me in her album,' was his comment.

'Sure she does. You're a dish,' answered Joanne, laughing.

'Thank you, ma'am, but you know what they say . . . *chacun à son goût*,' he said, looking at Cassandra with his inscrutable expression.

'If you move more to the left I can get in some surf dashing against those black rocks at the end of the beach,' said Joanne, with a gesture indicating where she wanted them to stand.

Trying to look casual about it, Cassandra moved to the spot and stood with her feet apart and her hands loosely clasped in front of her. She didn't expect Nick to put his arm round her, and he didn't.

'Hey, don't look so serious, both of you! Big smiles . . . say cheese or brush,' Joanne instructed.

As Cassandra pinned on a smile, Nick moved closer and rested his hand on the top of her shoulder.

Being in love was like taking mescalin or one of the other drugs said to heighten perception, she thought. If Harley or Hugh or Chris had put their hands on her shoulder in similar circumstances, she wouldn't have felt each finger as a separate entity and their exact position imprinted on her bare skin.

They seemed to stand there for minutes before Joanne pressed the button and the picture was taken.

'I'll have these developed right away. Fiji is a duty-free place, isn't it, Nick? I might buy one of those cameras which print the pictures as you take them.'

He said, 'You might get a bargain in Fiji, but I'm inclined to believe that with any expensive equipment it's generally wiser to buy it from a reputable shop in one's home town. Then, if anything goes wrong, there's some comeback.'

His sea-cooled hand was still on Cassandra's shoulder, the thumb near the base of her neck. As he spoke to Joanne, he rubbed it lightly back and forth. It was, she felt sure, a movement as slight and unconscious as someone drumming their fingers on a table-top while deep in thought.

But it had an effect on her more disturbing than if another man had caressed the whole length of her spine. If Nick could make her insides melt with a small movement of his thumb, what unimaginable bliss would she have experienced if she had spent a whole night in his arms?

Oh, lucky, lucky Joanne who, if she hadn't as yet, soon would be spending her nights with him, she thought, with a pang of envy.

She moved away, leaving them talking about cameras.

The next day there was an expedition further along the coast to Oheo Gulch where, in a series of waterfalls and pools, a stream made its way from the thickly forested heights of the interior to the ocean. Near the beach where the fresh water merged with the surf, there was a large open headland with views along the rugged coast. The whole area was part of the Haleakala National Park and permission had been obtained from the Park Rangers for *Ocean Wanderer*'s chefs to cook lunch on portable barbecues which, apparently, were among Harley's innovations.

Later, when lunch was over and the passengers had dispersed to explore the paths through the woods or to photograph the Seven Sacred Pools, Cassandra found a place on the headland where, with a boulder for a backrest, she could sit on the warm turf, watching the Pacific.

She was surprised when Harley joined her. 'All on your own, Cassandra?'

It was the kind of remark which would have prompted a sarcastic rejoinder from Professor Vernon. She, although she didn't welcome Harley's intrusion, smiled and said, 'I was thinking about the first settlers coming here from the South Pacific on outrigger canoes, not knowing if they would ever make landfall. All those unimaginable miles of ocean—and not always as calm as it is today.'

'I guess there had to be something pretty bad going on where they came from to make them set out on a voyage into the unknown,' he agreed. 'Rosie tells me you're not too happy about her and me. Is that right?'

His bluntness did more than startle her. It had never crossed her mind that Ros would tell him how she felt, and she was taken aback by Harley raising the subject with her.

He watched her, waiting for her to say something.

After some hesitation, she decided to match his directness.

'I suppose it's not really my business, except that I feel uncomfortable accepting your hospitality when you're not, as I thought, going to be my future brother-in-law. Also it worries me that Ros is in a situation which can't bring her lasting happiness.'

'You'd like to see her married and settled down, hm?'

'Either that or earning her living in a satisfying job.'

Harley contemplated the white-flecked dark blue surface of the deep ocean, outside the reef, for a few moments.

'Cassandra, you're making the mistake, which we all do when we're young, of judging everyone by yourself. I've known you long enough to tell you're an intelligent girl, a potential career girl. Rosie isn't. She doesn't have brains and, if she had, she's too lazy to use them. I don't mean that unkindly. Don't get angry with me for stating the facts. She has a great figure and a pretty face, but there's not as much between her ears, as they say, as there is between yours.'

'There are plenty of interesting jobs which don't call for a college education.'

'Maybe so, but they usually require initiative and drive, and your sister doesn't have those qualities. As I said, she's lazy. She likes getting up late and taking an hour to do her face. The only energetic thing she enjoys is dancing. She would hate a nine-to-five job in an office or a department store, and I don't think she's suited to being a suburban housewife. It's not easy to keep a house nice and cook meals day after day and raise kids the right way. It's not as tough as it was when my mother was doing it, but it's still a lot of hard work and responsibility. Can you see Rosie not buying a dress she wanted because her kids needed new shoes, or getting up early to fix their breakfasts and pack their lunch pails? Maybe you can. I can't.'

Cassandra's eyes held a sparkle of anger as she said, 'She was very good to me when I was little. If a man really loved her, clothes might become less important to her.'

'They might, but I doubt it. The way she looks is her greatest interest in life—as it is to a lot of women.'

'She won't always be young and pretty. What will become of her then, if she goes on like this?'

'That's a long time ahead. It's not my problem and it's not yours either, Cassandra. You can't change her and you shouldn't worry about her. We can only change our own lives. I learned that when my kids were growing up. It's no use trying to plan other people's lives for them, or getting upset when they go their own way.'

His attitude made her feel entitled not to mince words.

'I wonder if you'd be as philosophical about it if you had a daughter who was living with a man old enough to be her father,' she said bluntly.

'One of my daughters has a boy-friend who isn't as old as I am, but he's forty and has a wife and three kids. It's not a situation which makes me happy, but I have to accept that Julie is a grown woman and if that's what she wants, I have no right to interfere. I didn't make a great job of my own life. I married too young and for the wrong reasons; the chief one being that it wasn't easy to get a girl into bed in those days, not even for the good-looking guys.'

When she remained silent, he went on, 'As for the moral aspect, your sister isn't doing anything worse than the wife who stays with her husband, after she's stopped feeling any affection for him, because he's the chief breadwinner and it's easier to put up with him than to manage on her own. Before you condemn your sister, think about how many women stay married for convenience, and ask yourself where's the difference between them and Rosie.'

'*I* don't condemn my sister,' she exclaimed indignantly. 'I just hate her to be thought——' She left the sentence unfinished, unwilling to use any of the derogatory terms which she suspected others on board had applied to Rosalind.

'Do you hate it for her, or for yourself because you feel what people think about her affects how they think about you?' he asked shrewdly.

A few days later Cassandra had her first experience of lying in bed listening to the throbbing of the ship's engines. It was the last sound she heard before she slept, and the first to penetrate her consciousness in the morning.

A large chart of the Pacific between Hawaii and Fiji had been set up in the saloon. Each day their progress was marked on it. During those first days at sea she had several conversations with Atu, and seeing her interest in the chart, he would take a few minutes from his duties to point out a group of islands and tell her about them, sometimes describing an adventure which he and Nick had had there when they were schoolboys, spending their holidays together on Captain Ted's freighter *Tagimoucia*.

'What does *Tagimoucia* mean?' Cassandra asked him, the first time he mentioned the name of Nick's father's ship.

'It means "crying tears of despair",' said the Chief Steward.

'What a strange name for a ship!'

'It's also the name of a very rare flower which grows

on one of our islands. Not on all of them; only on Taveuni, and not everywhere there. It grows by a lake, four thousand feet above the sea, in the crater of a dormant volcano.

'There's a legend about it,' he went on. 'There was once a Fijian chief's daughter who was in love with a young man, but her father had decided to marry her to an old one. She ran away into the forest and wandered about for a long time. Eventually, almost exhausted, she came to the shores of a lake where she made herself a bed of vines and lay down to rest. When a search party from her village found her, she was crying in her sleep. As her tears fell on the vines, they changed into crimson flowers. Meanwhile her father had relented, and it was the young man she loved who woke her up.'

'What a lovely story,' said Cassandra, smiling. 'Have you ever seen the flowers, Atu?'

He nodded. 'They're very beautiful. It's a tradition in Fiji that a bouquet of *tagimoucia* is given to visiting royalty. If you want to see what they're like, ask the Captain to show you the painting of them in his cabin. His mother painted it. She loved flowers. There's a room in the house where the Captain stays when he's in Sydney which is full of her paintings. The last one she ever did was of *tagimoucia*. Captain Ted went to Taveuni specially to get the flowers for her. Soon after that her illness got worse and she couldn't paint any more. It wasn't long before she died. I think, when he was alone, Captain Ted spent many hours "crying tears of despair",' Atu ended, his usually cheerful expression replaced by a sombre one.

As she thought of the spiritual anguish which Mrs Carroll must have suffered at knowing her time was running out and she would never see Nick grow to manhood, Cassandra's throat tightened.

Atu saw her eyes film with tears which she blinked away. He said, 'Now I've made you sad. Captain Nick says it isn't long since your father died. I'm sorry to have reminded you of your own loss.'

It surprised her that Nick should have mentioned her father's death to Atu. Several times that day she puzzled over it; wondering how such an unlikely subject had cropped up in the talks the two men had in private.

Harley's conversation with her was something else which had occupied her mind many times since the barbecue ashore. At first she had been annoyed by his uncomplimentary assessment of Rosalind's character and by his suggestion that Cassandra's objection to their relationship was partially motivated by self-interest.

However, thinking it over, she had come to accept that perhaps his judgment of Ros was sounder than her own; and that it *was* partly because of the feeling that she shared some of Rosalind's discredit, particularly in Nick's eyes, that she minded her sister's position as the owner's girl-friend.

One afternoon, she was sunbathing on the foredeck with several of the other women, pretending to doze but actually trying to straighten out some of her woollier ideas about life and love, when a tremendous clangour caused all the recumbent bodies to shoot into a sitting position.

'My God! What's that?' exclaimed Joanne.

'Ooh ... what a noise!' Norma protested, clapping her hands over her ears and wincing at the loud continuous sound.

'I think it's the signal to practise abandoning ship,' said Cassandra, raising her voice to be heard above the bell.

'Maybe it's for real,' said Joanne, looking alarmed.

'Not very likely on a calm sea in daylight,' Cassandra said, smiling reassuringly. 'Do you know what to do? We have to go to our cabins for our lifejackets. Then we have to go to our lifeboat stations.'

'Where's that?' asked Joanne.

'It will tell you where yours is on the notice on the inside of your cabin door,' Cassandra answered, rather astonished Joanne hadn't bothered to read it.

Rosalind's reaction, if inelegant, at least wasn't panicky. 'Oh, damn! What a bore. Typical of Captain Bligh to ruin our siestas. Why couldn't we do it before lunch if we have to do it at all?'

'He could have chosen four o'clock in the morning,' said her sister.

'Harley would have had something to say about that,' was Rosalind's comment, before they went to their cabins.

None of them, Cassandra realised on her way below, had thought to look up at the bridge where they might have seen something to indicate if the drill were merely an exercise or, as Joanne put it, 'for real'.

It seemed to her very improbable that, on a private yacht, a fire could break out between decks and take hold to a dangerous extent before the passengers knew of it.

However, on the remote chance that it might be more than a routine test of the crew's efficiency and the passengers' common-sense, she thought quickly what she would do if the rest of the day, perhaps longer, had to be spent in a lifeboat.

It seemed to her that the first discomfort they would suffer, without shade or protective clothing, would be too much sun. Her sun-cream and sunglasses were already in her hand. Thrusting them into a beach bag, she flung on her father's dress shirt and a pair of white cotton pants she had bought before they left Lahaina.

Finally, as an afterthought, when she had put on her lifejacket, she dragged the sheets off the bed and bundled them under her arm.

The bell had stopped clanging and one of the junior stewards was rapping on the doors of other cabins and calling out, 'Everyone to lifeboat stations, please,' when she stepped on to the walkway.

'Is it a practice?' she asked him.

'Yes, miss, but if we don't do it in good time, the Captain say do it again.'

The practice didn't include lowering the boats over the side; clearly its purpose was mainly to test the passengers' reactions. Soon after they had assembled at their various stations, Nick and Hugh came round on a tour of inspection.

By this time Cassandra was beginning to feel rather foolish about her precautionary measures, especially bringing the sheets. These, during the few minutes' wait, she had folded and rolled up more neatly.

'You decided there was time to dress, I see,' remarked Nick, looking her over. The two other women at her station were in bathing suits.

'I thought, in a real emergency, I would need to protect myself from sunburn. It only took half a minute to fling on some clothes,' she explained.

'Did you think it was a real emergency?'

'Not really ... but I wasn't one hundred per cent sure.'

'What did you bring the sheets for?'

Cassandra was beginning to feel she had made an idiot of herself. 'To protect other people from burning ... as coverings or even as awnings. I——'

Nick turned away to speak to one of the other women. Hugh smiled at her and said, 'You needn't wait, Cassandra. Tea will be served on the top deck in a few minutes.'

It was about a quarter of an hour later, when everyone was having tea, that the two senior officers joined them and Hugh called for silence.

'The Captain would like your attention for a few moments, ladies and gentlemen.'

Nick stepped forward. 'I'm sorry it was necessary to

interrupt your normal activities this afternoon, ladies and gentlemen, but I'm sure you understand the wisdom of rehearsing what you should do in the event of our having to leave the ship. That is, I assure you, a most unlikely contingency as long as you all observe the regulations about smoking. However, before I thank you for your co-operation, I should like to point out that, in the event of your having to abandon ship on this or any other cruise, the last thing to worry about is the safety of valuables such as jewellery. Your first concern should always be your own safety and that of others. I'm sure no one on *Ocean Wanderer* would be as foolish as the passenger who, in a serious emergency on a large liner some years ago, attempted to pack a suitcase. But not everyone here behaved as sensibly as the youngest of the ladies on board.'

Until he turned his head to look at her, Cassandra didn't grasp who he meant.

His gaze didn't stay on her long. With a sweeping glance round the rest of his audience, he continued, 'Cassandra was one of the first to arrive at her lifeboat station, but, because she wasn't certain the drill was an exercise, she had taken sensible measures. She had put on some clothes to protect her body from the sun. She had brought sheets because it had struck her that others might have no protection. I'd like to congratulate her on her commendable good sense.'

This time when he looked at her, he smiled.

In her whole life Cassandra couldn't remember such a wonderful surprise as being publicly praised by the man whose good opinion meant so much to her. For a few moments, basking in his smile, she forgot about Joanne, forgot everything but the lovely sensation of winning his approval.

'Well done, Cassandra!' said Harley, leading a round of applause.

Whereupon her pleasure changed to embarrassment.

Blushing, she was relieved when, by turning away to the tea table, Nick indicated that his short speech was over.

'Count yourself honoured. It's not often the Skipper sings anyone's praises. Verbal lashings are his speciality,' murmured Chris, from behind her.

As she turned to him, smiling, such an odd, startled expression crossed his face that she asked, 'What's the matter?'

'I—I hadn't realised how pretty you are. No, that's not what I mean,' he corrected himself. 'You've always been pretty, but somehow today you look more so.'

'Thank you,' she smiled. 'I expect it's because I'm getting browner. By comparison with the rest of you, I looked quite ill when I arrived. It must be nice to live in the sun all the year round.'

'Wait till you've spent time in Fiji before you decide about that,' said another male voice, again speaking from close behind her.

This time her heart gave a lurch. She swivelled to look up at Nick. 'Is it much hotter in Fiji than in Hawaii?' she asked.

'It's a very hot, humid climate, which is great for lotus-eating but somewhat taxing for other purposes. You may find it saps your energy, mental as well as physical. Or you may thrive on it. How about getting Cassandra another cup of tea, Knight?'—this with a hint of reproof for his junior officer's failure to notice her cup was empty.

'Yes, sir. I'm sorry, Cassandra.' Chris took her cup and saucer and headed for the tea-table.

It was just as well Mrs Shane had put her in the picture about Nick's serious interest in Joanne, thought Cassandra. Otherwise she might have deluded herself that he was warming towards her. First that unexpected public accolade, and now this seeking her out and sending Chris off on an errand.

It was a delusion which would have been fostered by

his next move. He cupped a palm under her elbow and steered her away from the people standing near them.

Out of earshot of the others, he said, 'Thank you for taking the advice I gave you recently.'

'I still can't believe there was any danger of what you thought might happen,' she said, in a low voice. 'But mulling it over, I realised you must be the best judge of possible complications.

'Much the best judge,' he agreed. 'And before you accuse me of sexist arrogance and strike a feminist attitude, let me add that I only meant that you underestimate your effect on the male sex. Judging by what I overheard a minute ago, you've got young Knight's head in a whirl. Well, that won't do him any harm. It's a natural state at his age.'

He paused, his mouth curving slightly in a way she found deeply disturbing.

'Even Atu, who generally doesn't have much to say in praise of women, tells me you're a very nice girl.'

'How kind of him,' said Cassandra, thinking: What a strange thing for him to say unless you were saying something against me. 'I seem to be in everyone's good books at the moment—even yours,' she added.

'You——'

But whatever he had intended to reply remained unspoken. Just then Chris came back with her cup and a plate of the small, delicious sandwiches which were served every day at tea-time.

If Nick had wanted to pursue their tête-à-tête, it would have been very easy for him to drain his own tea-cup and send Chris away a second time. But only a man in love went to lengths of that sort. Devoutly as she longed for him to love her, she knew it was wishful thinking.

He had his eye on Joanne, although Cassandra wasn't convinced it was a loving eye but rather that of a man who felt it was time to take a wife and, in the elegant American, had found a woman who measured up to his requirements.

As *Ocean Wanderer* approached the Fijian archipelago, the first chart was replaced with another showing the two largest islands, Vanua Levu and Viti Levu, and the many small islands around them, some forming groups, some remote from their neighbours.

When Cassandra set foot in Fiji, it was on an untrodden beach of pale powdered coral sand lapped by crystal-clear shallows shading from aquamarine to deep purple above the corals.

Later, when she had left the others and wandered off on her own, sometimes paddling in the warm sea, sometimes leaving a trail of footprints on the tide-washed sand between the water's edge and the drifts of sea-shells, she was reminded of the books from Aunt Esmée's childhood which she had kept at the cottage and Cassandra had read there. *Robinson Crusoe*, *Treasure Island*, *Swiss Family Robinson*, and a later best-seller considered rather shocking in its day, *The Blue Lagoon* by H. de Vere Stacpoole.

She had read them, curled up by the fire on cold winter afternoons, never dreaming that one day she would tread a coral strand and swim in a sea which felt like silk against her skin.

As the yacht cruised a leisurely passage in the direction of Suva, the modern capital of Fiji, her pleasure in the beauty of each new anchorage was enhanced by a feeling that Mrs Shane might be wrong about Nick's interest in Joanne.

If the stewardess were right, why didn't he spend more time with her?

One evening, just before dinner, Cassandra saw Joanne resisting Norma's efforts to lead her to his end of the table. Instead she sat next to Hugh and after dinner they danced together, often enough for

Cassandra to wonder if they might be developing a special interest in each other.

A few days later other people began to notice and comment on the amount of time they spent together.

Norma didn't approve. In Cassandra's hearing, she said to Harley, 'I don't know why Joanne has to waste her time with Hugh Davis, who's never going to be more than a second fiddle. Nick Carroll is much more suitable, and he seemed interested until she started this crazy romance with Hugh. How much do you pay him, Harley? She hasn't any money of her own, you know.'

There was no risk of her remarks being overheard by either of the officers concerned. The ship was under way and they were both on duty. Norma knew Cassandra was nearby and she hadn't bothered to lower her voice. Even so, Cassandra felt it was a private conversation, and she moved away without hearing Harley's reply. In the light of his remarks to her, she thought he would probably have told his cousin that her friend's relationship with Hugh was not her concern.

Shortly before they reached Suva, Cassandra discovered that Mrs Shane had an electric sewing machine. This gave her the idea of trying to copy some of the simple separates she had liked in the shop at Kapalua Bay. While the other women passengers were buying ready-to-wear clothes from Tiki Togs in the capital's main street, she was exploring the side streets where there were many Indian-owned shops selling fabrics for dresses and saris.

Fiji's international airport was near Nadi, at the other end of the island. After two days at Suva for Christmas shopping they cruised along the south coast to disembark the passengers who were flying back to America for Christmas and to collect new arrivals.

'It seems you were wrong, Mrs Shane . . . about those wedding bells you forecast,' said Cassandra, the afternoon they were due to berth at Lautoka, a small port not far from the airport.

She was using the sewing machine in the linen store where the stewardess ironed clothes. Steam-pressing of towels and bed linen was done in the ship's laundry.

'I'm not sure I follow you, Miss Cassandra,' said Mrs Shane.

'Don't you remember telling me you thought this cruise would end with a wedding ... the Captain's wedding?'

'Yes, I believe I did say something like that. What makes you think I was wrong?' the little Australian woman asked, with rather a beady sideways glance.

Perhaps she was not too pleased that her judgment of Nick's intentions had been mistaken. But if Cassandra had committed a gaffe by mentioning the matter, she couldn't drop the subject now.

'Like you, I thought the Captain and Mrs Walters seemed very well suited,' she said. 'But now it seems more likely she may marry Mr Davis.'

'Mrs Walters and Captain Nick? Oh, no, I never thought that,' was the stewardess's prompt response. 'She seems a very nice lady, but she's not right for him—not at all.'

She left Cassandra to ponder this statement while she took an expensive dress back to its owner's cabin.

The meaning of her last remark became clear a few hours later. By that time the yacht was alongside a wharf at Lautoka. Cassandra was on the upper deck, leaning over the rail to watch the activities below her and wondering if there was time to stroll into town before dinner.

Before she had made up her mind, she saw Nick coming round the corner of a building further along the quay. He was carrying a document case, and she concluded he had been attending to some formalities.

As he approached the boarding ramp which had been

set up between the quay and the lower deck, a taxi drew up alongside it. The rear door opened and out swung a pair of long shapely dark brown legs followed by the rest of a tall girl in a white blouse and pink cotton skirt.

Cassandra had seen a great many pretty girls in the streets of Suva; the Fijians were a handsome people. But this girl was more than pretty. She was beautiful, with a grace of movement and a patrician air which made an immediate impact.

'Nick!' Her glad cry had nothing raucous about it.

He had been striding along with a preoccupied frown. At the sight of her this changed to a look of delight.

'Eleni!' He stopped short, looking as if she were the most welcome sight he had seen in a long time.

As she ran to him, his arms opened to envelop her in the most loving hug Cassandra had ever witnessed.

It was a painful experience to see Eleni being held in the arms which had once embraced her. She could hardly bear to watch yet she found it impossible to turn away.

Then Eleni drew back a little. Although Cassandra couldn't see her expression, she could hear the joy in her voice as she said to him, 'This is going to be the happiest Christmas of my life, Nick. Even if my father hadn't relented, I should have come. It's taken a long, long time, but at last I've made him understand there's only one man for me.'

CHAPTER SIX

CASSANDRA had never warmed to Terry Anson, and shortly before dinner that evening, her attitude to him crystallised into active hostility.

He strolled over to where she was sitting with her sister, and said, 'Have you seen the new stewardess? She's a good-looking piece. I wonder which of the stewards will have her for his Christmas present. My bet's on Atu.' He gave an unpleasant laugh.

'Just because you regard all women as sex objects, it doesn't follow that the stewards do,' she said coldly. 'If I had to be marooned with anyone, I'd feel a lot safer with Atu or David or Josaia than I would with you.'

As she stood up and walked away, she heard him say angrily, 'Stuck-up little bitch! I don't know why you bother with her, Ros.'

Soon after supper Cassandra went to her cabin. With Christmas now only two days away and everyone else in high spirits, it was hard to join in the merriment when her own heart was aching with a love which would never be returned.

She had been in her cabin no more than five or ten minutes when, without knocking, Rosalind burst in.

'What the hell do you mean by being so bloody insulting to Terry before dinner?' she demanded, after slamming the door.

'It was he who was insulting to Eleni,' said Cassandra coldly.

'He was only joking.'

'Then it was in very bad taste, and it's just as well Nick didn't hear him. *He* would have told Terry off much more strongly than I did.'

Rosalind's blue eyes glittered with irritation. 'You've no right to tell him off at all. Who do you think you are? You seem to forget your position. You're damned lucky to be here. I don't expect you to repay me by being rude to my friends!'

'I'm very much aware of my position, Ros. I shouldn't have come, and the sooner I go the better. I'll see about it tomorrow.'

Her sister glowered for some seconds. Then she said, 'Don't be silly. I didn't mean that. Anyway, you've nowhere to go.'

'I have. I can go back to England.'

'Why do you want to go back to that awful climate? I'm never going to if I can help it. Europe is old and played out. America and maybe Australia is where the action is now.'

'Perhaps—I don't know,' shrugged Cassandra. 'But I do have some contacts in England and I think I can get a place at university, which I shouldn't be able to in America or Australia.'

Rosalind, her outburst over, was beginning to show the boredom which was always her reaction when Cassandra spoke of resuming her studies.

'Harley will be wondering where I am. Aren't you coming on deck again?' she asked.

'No, I think I'll stay here and read.'

'Oh, well, suit yourself. Good night.'

After she had gone Cassandra decided that instead of reading she would go to the linen store and do some more dressmaking. If her time on board was nearly at an end, she must try to make up the fabrics more quickly than she had intended.

Machining the seams she had basted earlier allowed her to think what to do. It would look strange if she left the yacht before Christmas. She would have to remain until the festivities were over and leave at the end of the Christmas cruise through the Yasawa group of islands.

Many of the passengers would be going home then and her departure would cause no comment.

She had taken her foot off the pedal and was hand-finishing the lines of machined stitches when she heard voices in the corridor. The door was closed, but there was a louvred panel inset in the bottom part of it which admitted sounds from outside.

With the sudden tensing which the sound of his voice always caused, she heard Nick say, 'I wish you could have one of the passenger cabins. Compared with some ships, the accommodation for deck crew and cabin staff isn't at all bad. But it's not what you're used to, Eleni.'

'I don't mind. I'd sleep in a chain locker if necessary.' There was a soft musical laugh. 'I was beginning to despair of us ever being together. My parents are still hoping against hope that propinquity will open my eyes to all kinds of incompatibilities I hadn't noticed before. But they've reached the stage of accepting that I'm never going to marry any of their choices for me, so it's this or no marriage at all.'

'For you not to marry would be——' Nick's voice, close now, broke off. 'Someone's left the light on in there ... unless Shaney's still working. She ought to be off duty now.'

The door of the linen store opened.

'Oh, it's you, Cassandra.' He pushed the door wider open. 'Have you met our new stewardess? This is Eleni Tavaga, who's going to be helping Mrs Shane until we reach Sydney.'

Cassandra put aside her sewing and stood up and held out her hand. 'How do you do? I'm Cassandra Vernon.'

At close quarters the Fijian girl was even more lovely than she had looked at a distance. Her head was poised on a long neck and she had very large dark brown eyes framed by curling black lashes. But it wasn't perfection of feature alone which made her a beauty, but the sweetness of her expression.

Cassandra could well understand why Nick had fallen in love with her and been prepared to wait years for her parents' opposition to weaken.

He said, 'You look very busy. What are you making?'

'I'm trying to copy some clothes which I saw in Maui, but I'm not a very expert dressmaker. Are you a needlewoman, Miss Tavaga?'

'Yes, I like sewing very much.'

'Eleni is clever with her hands. She's a talented painter,' said Nick.

'No, not talented, but I enjoy it,' said Eleni. 'I once tried my hand at sculpture. Nick was on leave in Sydney and I persuaded him to sit for me. The result was terrible! I made you look like a monster from another planet, didn't I?' she said, laughing.

'It wasn't flattering,' he agreed.

The smile which lit his grey eyes made it very clear to Cassandra how their love affair must have begun. This lovely girl, far from home and probably missing her family and friends, would have exercised all Nick's best instincts.

As if it had struck her that her manner towards him had been too familiar for a newly appointed stewardess, even one who had known him elsewhere, Eleni said more sedately, 'Captain Carroll's relations were very kind to me while I was in Australia.'

'Miss Vernon is English,' said Nick. 'This is her first visit to the Pacific.'

His use of her surname, underlining the pretence that Eleni was a *bona fide* member of the crew, made Cassandra wonder how he would contain his fury if any of the passengers treated her less than courteously. Not that he was likely to be present if and when it happened, and no doubt Eleni would keep it to herself if the masquerade carried some penalties for her.

'I hope you're enjoying it, Miss Vernon,' the Fijian girl said politely.

'I'd have to be very hard to please if I weren't,' said Cassandra, in answer to her remark. 'I thought Maui was lovely, but Fiji is even more beautiful. You were lucky to be born in such a marvellous part of the world, Miss Tavaga.'

Before Eleni could answer, Nick reminded her that she hadn't finished turning down the passengers' beds.

'No, I have three more to do. Good night, Miss Vernon.' Giving Cassandra another of her ravishing smiles, she hurried away to carry on with her duties.

Instead of following her, Nick lingered in the doorway.

'Eleni is new to this job, so it will take her a few days to master it. The Fijians aren't people who can be rushed,' he said dryly. 'In their climate hustle and bustle isn't practical, as I expect you've discovered ashore.'

'I did find I had to stroll around Suva at a more leisurely pace than my usual one,' she agreed.

'What did you think of the place?'

'It has a wonderful museum, although it's just as well Norma didn't go there. I think she'd have been almost as horrified by the carved wooden forks which the chiefs used for eating human flesh as she was by that rat at the market. It's extraordinary how, in only a few generations, the Fijians have changed from fierce warriors to civilised, friendly men like Atu.'

His mouth quirked. 'Don't be misled by Atu's sunny smile. Most of the time he's as gentle as a lamb. But I've known a couple of occasions when he's lost his temper and I was very glad not to be on the receiving end of it.'

For some time after he had left her, she went on with her dressmaking. When she returned to her cabin, it occurred to her that although the passengers' quarters were well supplied with reading matter, Eleni's cabin might not be.

Selecting several books and magazines which she thought might interest the other girl, she went to find her.

The deck below the passengers' quarters was a part of the ship she had never ventured in before. As she was standing in the long corridor at the foot of the companionway, wondering which way to go, the Chief Steward appeared.

'Atu, where will I find the new stewardess . . . Eleni?' she asked him.

For the first time since she had known him, the Fijian didn't smile at her.

'If you want Eleni, you should ring your bell, Miss Cassandra,' he said, in a strange tone of voice.

'I don't want her to do anything for me. I want to offer her these books in case she has nothing to read in her cabin. She may find it difficult to sleep, her first night on board.'

Although if she does lie awake, her thoughts will be happy ones, was her unspoken rider.

To her astonishment, Atu said angrily, 'She shouldn't be on board—except as an honoured guest. She's the daughter of an important chief. It isn't fitting for her to work as a stewardess. It was wrong of Nick to allow this foolishness.'

Cassandra had never seen him in anything but a good mood before. Nor had he ever referred to his friend as other than 'the Captain'. It was a measure of his mood that he had done so now. He looked as annoyed as Nick had been the night he had hauled her out of the water and berated her in terms he would never normally use to a woman.

Not knowing what to say, she was silent.

With a visible effort the Fijian mastered his displeasure. 'I'll show you her cabin.' He turned and strode down the corridor, moving lightly for so large a man.

Outside Eleni's cabin he rapped on the door. They heard her say, 'Come in.'

Atu said something in Fijian. A moment later the door opened and Eleni appeared. She was wrapped in a *sulu* the colour of coral. The vivid colour flattered her dark skin. Her bare shoulders gleamed in the light coming from behind her. She had a flower in her hair; a peach-coloured hibiscus with a blood-red centre. Had Nick put it there?

She looked surprised to see Atu. Then she noticed Cassandra standing behind him.

'Miss Cassandra wishes to speak to you.' He continued on down the passage, which had another companionway at the far end.

Eleni's large dark brown eyes followed him for a few seconds before she turned to the other girl.

'Please come in, Miss Cassandra.'

The cabin was very much smaller than Cassandra's spacious accommodation. Whatever belongings Eleni had brought on board with her had been stowed away. The only personal possession which Cassandra noticed at first glance was a large framed photograph on the nightstand.

'Are those your parents?' she asked.

'Yes, and my brothers and sister when we were younger.' Eleni picked up the photograph and offered her a closer look.

Seated at the centre of the family group was a distinguished-looking grey-haired man.

'Your father is a *ratu*, I believe?' said Cassandra.

Eleni looked startled. 'Did Ni—Captain Carroll tell you that?'

'No, Atu did just now. I gather he doesn't approve of your present rôle.'

Eleni replaced the photograph before she said, 'The Fijian class system is difficult for people from other cultures to understand. A police constable may be a *ratu*, or a barman in an hotel may be a *ratu*. His village still owns the land on which the hotel is built and he and his people are also entitled to work in the hotel if they wish. If a *ratu* can work as a barman, there's no reason why I shouldn't be a stewardess. Atu has some rigid ideas about what is done and not done. Please sit down.'

· She drew out the upright chair which had had its seat tucked under the bracket table which doubled as a dressing-table and desk.

'Thank you. I hope you don't mind my bursting in on you like this, but it suddenly struck me you might have nothing to read which, for me, is a fate worse than death. None of these books may interest you, but anything to read is better than nothing, don't you think?'

Eleni nodded vigorously. 'Yes, I do. How thoughtful of you, Miss Vernon.'

'Look, if you want to keep up a pretence in public, that's okay by me, but couldn't we drop it in private?' Cassandra suggested. 'I know you're really a teacher—Mr Shane mentioned it.'

'I see.' Eleni looked thoughtfully at her. 'Yes, teaching is what I've been doing for several years, but I wouldn't say it was my true vocation.' She paused again, and Cassandra intuitively recognised that she was debating with herself how much to confide.

'What did you really want to do?' she asked.

'I wanted to marry and have children,' Eleni confessed. 'And you, Cassandra? What will you do with your life?'

'I'm not sure.' She wondered if Eleni knew that her sister was the owner's girl-friend. Perhaps she didn't yet. When she found out, she might be horrified and the rapport between them which Cassandra had been aware of from the moment Nick introduced them would be spoiled.

It was strange how, although the Fijian girl had put paid to the last faint hope that a miracle would happen and Nick would suddenly realise that Cassandra was his heart's desire, she could not help liking and being drawn to Eleni.

'My problem,' said the other girl, 'was that I knew what I wanted—or rather *who* I wanted—too soon. I've been in love with him since I was fifteen and although, if they had known, everyone would have told me it wouldn't last and I should grow out of it, it has lasted. But even if there had been no barriers between us, my parents wouldn't have wanted me to marry too young. With the obstacles which do exist, it's taken a long time to convince them I'll never look at anyone else.'

'But surely, as a man, they must like and admire him, don't they?'

'Yes, they do. They know all his good qualities. But they would still prefer me to marry one of the sons of their friends, and to live the same kind of life my mother has had. As well as looking after us, she's been very active in encouraging women to revive traditional skills which have been in danger of dying out.'

They went on talking for some time until Cassandra, realising it was getting late and that, while she had nothing much to do. Eleni had to work tomorrow, said good night.

Cassandra had waited in vain for Joanne to show her the prints from the roll of film she had used up at Hamoa Beach. Several times she had been tempted to remind the American woman. In the end she hadn't mentioned the matter for fear Joanne might suspect how much she longed to possess the photograph of herself with Nick.

On Christmas Day, Joanna presented each of her fellow passengers with a plastic cube paperweight into which could be slotted six photographs. In the cube she gave to Cassandra there were three snapshots; the one with Nick, another of Ros with Harley, and a picture of *Ocean Wanderer* at anchor in Lahaina Roads.

Everyone who received a cube was delighted with Joanna's clever idea. She was congratulated for having had the forethought to bring a box of them with her from California.

Harley's gifts were more lavish. He gave Rosalind a necklace which made her shriek with delight when she opened the case, and Cassandra cringe with concealed mortification as she watched him fasten the costly string of fine pearls round her sister's neck.

Further embarrassment was in store. Harley's present to Cassandra was a pendant on a fine gold chain. The pendant was a gold disc set with five diamonds representing the five stars of the Southern Cross. There was nothing she could do but pretend to be grateful for his generosity. But for the rest of the morning, until they all went swimming before lunch and she could take the thing off, she felt humiliated by it.

The presents which she gave people had had of necessity to be at the opposite end of the scale from the expensive gifts Harley bestowed on his guests. Like him, she had included the ship's officers and the cabin crew on her present-buying list. But it was a surprise to find that, with the exception of Terry Anson, all the officers had chosen a present for her.

She and Joanne were the only passengers who received presents from them, and most people on board could have predicted that Hugh would give Joanna a token of his increasingly obvious regard for her.

But why she should be singled out to receive presents from Chris, Hugh, George and Nick was beyond Cassandra's comprehension. Although she didn't understand it, she found it extraordinarily warming. And when she opened the wrapping on Nick's choice for her, she could have burst into tears, she was so much moved. Fortunately she was able to mask this reaction as she had hidden her other feelings. But later on, in her cabin, she couldn't help shedding a few tears as she tried on the *sulu* he had given her.

It was one of several she had received, but the others were the standard pieces of opaque cotton brightly patterned with hibiscus flowers, palm trees and similar South Seas motifs. Nick's choice was a *sulu* of semi-transparent fine voile printed with swirls of colour—deep sea-greens with streaks of indigo and amethyst—and criss-crossed with fine silver threads.

She decided to wear it for lunch. After Christmas she would put it away in tissue paper, to be taken out sometimes and fingered gently, like a wedding dress. For her, now, there would never be a wedding day, or a trousseau, or a honeymoon, or any of the bridal delights which, before coming on this cruise, she had taken for granted would be a part of her life.

Nick must like her much better than he had at first, or he wouldn't have selected this beautiful Christmas present for her. It showed an insight into her tastes of which, at the beginning of their relationship, she would have thought him incapable. But the fact remained that the man she loved was in love with someone else. That was unalterable.

Brushing away a large tear which had brimmed over her eyelid and trickled down her cheek, she made a resolute effort to batten down her emotions. It wouldn't do to appear at lunch with red eyes.

The evening before Nick had brought the yacht into a channel of deep water between two small uninhabited islands in the Yasawa chain. From both sides of the ship they looked out on pale golden beaches and thickets of palms.

Wearing the *sulu* draped round her in the way Eleni had worn her coral one, Cassandra left her cabin and made her way up to the saloon.

In the lagoon to starboard, the deck crew were all off duty and enjoying a swim. The two assistant stewards were with them because the passengers' lunch was to be a serve-yourself buffet of salads, presided over by Atu, to leave them with good appetites for a traditional Christmas dinner after dark.

Barefoot because, like wristwatches, shoes were superfluous on a cruise through these islands and most people wore them only if they had to walk on the sometimes burning hot sand, she started to climb the wide stairway to the upper deck.

There seemed hardly anyone about. Most of the passengers must still be changing. But she could hear two voices from the deck above. Because they were speaking Fijian, she didn't realise immediately that they weren't engaging in the usual cheerful chatter of the crew using their own language to converse among themselves.

As it dawned on her that an argument verging on a quarrel was in progress, instinct made her halt. She had no wish to intrude on a private spat.

Before she could retreat, a distressful protest from Eleni was interrupted by a tirade from Atu.

He was still in full spate when Eleni came flying down the stairway, her soft dark eyes brimming with tears as Cassandra's had not long before.

For a few moments after the Fijian girl had rushed past her and disappeared, she wondered whether to follow her. Then she thought it might be more useful to leave Eleni to cry in private and to stand up for her against Atu before anyone else arrived on the scene and the opportunity to tell him what she thought of him was lost.

Marching up the remaining stairs, she found the Chief Steward standing by the rails, apparently watching the other crew members at play in the sparkling lagoon. But the force with which he was gripping the topmost rail and the plum-coloured tinge of the skin of his strong dark neck hinted at repressed rage.

'Really, Atu, I think it's too bad of you to upset Eleni on Christmas Day!' she said hotly.

The Fijian swung round to face her, and for an instant she quailed before the ferocity of his expression. 'This is not your business, Miss Cassandra.'

'It isn't yours either,' she said. 'If Eleni's parents no longer object, what right have you to cast a blight on her happiness? True love, which has proved itself true as hers has, is more important than anything else in the world. If you have ever loved someone who ...' her voice shook '... who didn't love you, you wouldn't try to spoil things for her.'

The big Fijian stared at her in sombre silence.

From behind her, Nick's voice said quietly, 'Something wrong, Cassandra?'

It was a tradition, started by the previous owner who had spent many Christmases cruising, that on Christmas Day no one wore uniform. Like Atu, who was wearing a tailored grey *sulu* and grey linen sports shirt, Nick was in civilian clothes, but his were more casual than his friend's. His shirt was pink, tucked inside well-cut beige shorts. Today he wasn't wearing his usual white stockings. His brown feet were bare inside a pair of black leather sandals which, she had noticed in Suva, were more or less standard wear among Fijian men.

How long he had been there and how much he had heard was impossible to tell. Judging by his expression, he hadn't encountered Eleni. Cassandra had no intention of kindling bad feeling between him and his life-long friend, especially not on Christmas Day.

Mustering a smile, she said cheerfully, 'Not a thing. Where is everybody? I'm getting hungry, aren't you?'

His response was a noncommittal murmur before he added, 'It suits you'—looking at the gauzy *sulu*.

In the altercation with Atu, Cassandra had forgotten it. 'It's beautiful—I'm delighted with it. Thank you very much, Nick.'

Her present to him had been impersonal; a bottle of over-proof Fijian rum, the same as her gift to the Engineer.

'There's one thing missing,' he said.

At either end of the buffet table was an arrangement of flowers which must either have been kept fresh in cold storage or procured from some nearby island where there was a village. Nick selected a flower with white petals and a golden heart and came close to put it in her hair. He smelt of soap and clean clothes with a faint tinge of something else, either shampoo or a discreet shaving lotion.

Meltingly aware of his nearness, she said huskily, 'I haven't the right sort of hair for flowers. Eleni's is perfect. In her hair they stay put.'

'You have very nice hair.' As he placed the flower over her ear, his hand brushed her cheek. Even that brief, light touch sent deep shivers through her.

Nick stepped back to see the effect, and as his grey gaze moved downwards, she could almost believe she saw a fugitive glint of desire as he looked at the curves of her body lightly swathed in the filmy voile.

But the next thing he said made it clear that she had imagined it. He had been looking her over with the keen eye for detail of a commanding officer with perfectionist standards.

'You've forgotten to put on Mr Dennison's pendant,' he said quietly.

This time she knew it wasn't her imagination which read into his expression an understanding of her feelings about the pendant and a reminder that she was Harley's guest and must honour her obligation not to injure his feelings.

She nodded. 'I'll go and get it.'

That, even on Christmas Day, he wasn't prepared to overlook anything which conflicted with his views on correct conduct was demonstrated later on when she saw him say something in an undertone to the Radio Officer.

Earlier, seeing Terry in mufti had made her realise how a smart uniform could transform a man's appearance and give a false impression of the type of person he was. In his own clothes, Terry Anson looked much more brash and foxy than in his officer's rig.

He had come on deck wearing very tight white synthetic trousers and white patent loafers with a gilt trim. His aloha shirt was one of the most garish she had seen, and he had left several buttons open to show off two gold neck-chains, one of them longer than the other with a large medallion swinging from it. A flashy ring and a gold identity bracelet were two other pieces of jewellery he didn't normally wear. The total effect was that his natural milieu was a race-course or a club with a shady reputation. Even his hair had a styled look as if he had spent half an hour carefully blow-drying it into shape.

Her father's vanity, although of a different order from Terry's, had made Cassandra wary of men who took an inordinate interest in their appearance. She couldn't imagine Nick possessing a dryer. He would vigorously tousle his thick dark hair with a towel, brush or comb it back from his forehead and temples, and have it trimmed at regular intervals. Ten times as good-looking as Terry, he probably rarely looked at himself in a mirror except when he was shaving or trying on new clothes.

Following Nick's quiet aside, Terry disappeared for a while, and when he came back his shirt had only the top button unfastened. She saw him shoot a resentful look at Nick's broad back.

When Eleni reappeared her manner was composed

and she looked particularly lovely in a loose, halter-strapped sundress in shades of saffron and peach, two colours particularly becoming to the bistre tones of her skin.

She and Mrs Shane and the two chefs had their lunch with the passengers. Atu ate his behind the buffet table with Chris also there, chatting to him and helping him replenish people's glasses with champagne. The rest of the crew had a picnic lunch ashore in the shade of the coconut palms.

Very soon she would have to return to a workaday world which, in this present setting, seemed as remote and unreal as the South Pacific had seemed when she was nursing her father in Cambridge.

She thought about Nick and Eleni sharing the future on a schooner, perhaps one something like the coral-sailed schooner *Tui Tai* which had left Lautoka at the same time as *Ocean Wanderer*, ferrying a crowd of young people to Beachcomber Island.

Visualising their happy life together, she knew that whoever had coined the expression 'my heart bleeds' must have felt as she did today; as if, minute by minute, her own capacity for happiness was draining away; as if, all the time she was smiling and sipping champagne, she was dying inside.

Lunch was over and some people had gone below for a siesta while others were lingering over coffee and the apparently inexhaustible supply of champagne when Nick strolled over to where she was sitting with George Hendrikson.

'I'm off for a nap,' said the grey-bearded Engineer as the younger man joined them. He and Cassandra were sharing a two-seater white cane sofa. George said, 'See you later m'dear,' and gave her knee a paternal pat before vacating his place beside her.

As Nick took it over, he said, 'I'm going to clear my head with a swim. How about you?'

His friendly smile was a refinement of the torture of being close to him.

'I think I'd rather emulate George and perhaps have a swim later on,' she answered.

She would have risen, but Nick put a hand on her arm and stopped her. 'I couldn't help hearing part of what you were saying to Atu before lunch.'

As he paused, she tensed, wondering what was coming next.

'About love,' he added, as if she might have forgotten.

When she remained silent, he went on, 'You've changed a great deal since you joined us. Physically you're in much better shape. I'm referring to your health, not your figure,' he added, with a slight smile. 'There was never anything wrong with that, but you looked very white and worn out. Now you're tanned and rested. I'm sure you've never looked better, Except . . .' Once again he paused, his keen eyes searching her face. 'Except that I think there's still something on your mind.'

There was no one near them, but even so he dropped his voice a tone as he said, 'I don't think it's only concern for your sister, although I know that's one of your worries.'

She had turned her head to avoid his penetrating scrutiny. Now she flashed an uncertain glance at him.

'Blood isn't always thicker than water, I'm afraid. You'll have to face that. I would go as far as to say you have more in common with Eleni than with Rosalind.'

'I like Eleni very much,' she said, in a low voice. 'She's a lovely person.'

'I've always thought so,' he agreed. 'I'm glad you share my opinion. So does Atu at rock bottom, although you might not think so. But he'll come round in time, and then it'll be all plain sailing.'

If only he knew how hurtful this was to her. Thank God he didn't.

'I heard you tell Atu—and I'm glad you did—that love is the most important thing in life,' he went on. 'Am I right in thinking you were speaking from experience when you told Atu about the painful experience of loving and not being loved back?'

Was he talking about the past or the present? The possibility that he might have guessed how she felt about him was shattering.

Then, to her relief, he added. 'Was there . . . is there someone in England whom you're still missing, Cassandra?'

She jumped at the explanation. Anything was preferable to having him suspect the truth.

'Yes . . . yes, there is,' she said.

His brows drew together. 'I see. I thought that might be the reason. Well, you're very young and the chances are that in a few years' time you'll wonder what you saw in him. There are plenty of other pebbles on the beach, especially for a girl like you, with intelligence as well as looks.'

Somehow wishing she hadn't lied to him, even to save her pride, Cassandra said listlessly, 'I hope so.'

'Are you still planning to fly back to England from Fiji? Why not finish the cruise and see something of Australia?'

'I feel I've imposed on Harley too long as it is,' she answered. 'I should like to visit Australia, but not in my present circumstances as . . . as a free-loader.'

'I don't think Mr Dennison or anyone else regards you in that light. If you don't want to stay on board once we reach Sydney, I can fix you up on an *au pair* basis with one of my cousins' families. It's midsummer in Australia. Several of my cousins' wives are career-women who are always glad of extra help in the house, particularly during the school holidays, which go on till early February. You'd have a roof over your head, a little pin-money and time off for sightseeing. Think it over.'

'Yes . . . yes, I will. It's very kind of you to suggest it.'

He rose to his feet. Looking down at her, he said, 'It would make life pleasanter for Eleni to have you on board. She's in a difficult position at the moment. You know why she's helping Shaney. Having someone who knows the set-up to talk to would be a big help to her. Are you sure you won't change your mind about coming for a swim?'

There was nothing she would have liked more, but she shook her head.

'Okay. See you later.' Nick walked away.

Christmas night on board the yacht was a spectacular occasion, but it was the Fijian *meke* a few nights later which Cassandra found the more memorable.

The *meke*, an evening of songs and dances, was being given by the people of a village where the elderly chief had been a friend of Captain Ted and had known Nick all his life. The singing was to follow a feast provided by Nick and cooked in a *lovo*, a traditional underground oven, supervised by Atu.

Already staying on the island was an elderly Australian woman who had become friendly with an expatriate Fijian family in her native Queensland and was visiting their relations. She had come all the way from Lautoka sitting under a large umbrella on the deck of the small fishing boat which the islanders used to take produce to Viti Levu. The voyage had taken ten hours.

Miss Evans, as she introduced herself, reminded Cassandra of Aunt Esmée. She asked Harley's permission to bring her new friend on board for lunch and to offer her the chance of a hot shower which, although not necessary in that climate, was a pleasurable luxury, expecially for washing hair.

It was after Miss Evans had used Cassandra's shower and they were having a cup of tea together in the cabin that she startled Cassandra by saying, 'The Fijian couple you have on board are a very striking pair, aren't they? How long have they been married?'

'Atu and Eleni? They aren't married. What made you think they were?'

'The jealous way he keeps an eye on her,' said Miss Evans. 'When she was in the village this morning, a couple of the young men tried to chat her up, as they say now. Atu wasn't having that! They were sent off with a flea in their ear.

'You misunderstood him, Miss Evans. Eleni is ... spoken for, and Atu knows it. But he isn't the man in her life.'

'If he isn't, he'd like to be. Haven't you noticed the way he looks at her? You can't mistake love when you see it.' Miss Evans assured her, with the conviction of someone who knows she can't be mistaken.

By late afternoon the weather, which had been perfect since they entered Fijian waters, showed signs of fulfilling the morning's weather forecast of possible storms. In spite of the clouds overhead, the yacht party went ashore and the feast took place as planned, with everyone's plate piled high with good things from the *lovo*.

Most people had finished their meal before the first large drops of rain gave a few moments' warning of the deluge to follow. Among the Fijians the downpour was an occasion for cheerful exclamations among the adults as they hurried their visitors to shelter in their *bures*. To the children it was a great joke.

Harley and most of his guests took it in equally good part. Only Ros and a few other women who were very dressed up, were put out at having their hairdos reduced to rats'-tails and their finery drenched.

As the island had no *bure* large enough to accommodate everyone for the *meke*, and anyway most people were to wet to enjoy it without changing into dry clothes, as soon as the rain eased off the yacht party went back on board where the *meke* would be held later on.

An hour later, by which time the top afterdeck had been cleared for use as a stage, and the saloon and part of the central lounge deck had been filled with seating for the audience, the islanders and Miss Evans came on board. Those who were going to perform were dressed in costumes derived from the banana leaf or shredded hibiscus bark skirts and leafy anklets and bracelets of their ancestors.

They had brought with them many *leis* made from threaded frangipani flowers, mostly white but some pink and red. They had made one for Harley and each of his guests, and it must have taken a long time for the women of the island to pick and thread so many flowers without bruising the tender petals with their subtle fragrance.

As hers was placed gently on her shoulders by a girl of about her own age, and Cassandra murmured, 'Vinaka,' she knew that, for the rest of her life, the sight or scent of frangipani would evoke memories of the Pacific and Nick.

From where she was sitting she could see the back of his head and shoulders. He, too, wore a garland of flowers, and, as it did when Atu stuck a flower in his hair, the *lei* somehow served to emphasise Nick's masculinity.

The old chief began to conduct the first song, and she fixed her attention on the choir. They ranged from men and women in late middle-age to youths and girls in their teens.

After two songs they all sat down on the deck. The chief joined the men at the back in playing various simple wooden instruments while the women and girls, at the front, accompanied their singing with symbolic arm and hand movements. The rhythmic swaying of their bodies, the grace with which even stout matrons performed the fluid movements and, above all, the shy laughing glances which they exchanged with each other, made it a delightful performance which the audience applauded with enthusiasm.

Towards the end of the *meke*, Miss Evans, who was next to Cassandra, gave her a nudge with her elbow and, with a meaning look, directed her attention to Atu whom they could see from their seats. He was standing up, his arms folded. But he wasn't watching the islanders. His dark eyes were fixed on Eleni who, unaware of the burning gaze focused on her, was deeply absorbed in the music.

The Fijians ended their performance by singing the hauntingly lovely song of farewell *Isa Lei*. Then, after bowing his acknowledgment of the applause, the old chief went round shaking hands with everyone.

The people from the island didn't go home immediately but stayed to dance with the passengers to music played by some of the yacht's crew, two of whom were accomplished guitarists.

Nick hadn't danced with her on Christmas night and tonight he and the chief and Harley were drinking *aqgona* from a coconut cup. But Atu asked her to dance.

Certain now that Miss Evans was right and the girl he would have preferred to be holding in his arms was Eleni, Cassandra circled the deck with him in silence. She realised now that the reason for his angry reaction to Eleni's masquerade must be two-fold. Probably he did disapprove of the daughter of an important *ratu* having to take instructions from women who in social rank and personal qualities were inferior to her. But the major reason must be that her presence on board aggravated his longing for her.

'You're very quiet, Miss Cassandra,' he said, breaking into her thoughts.

'I wish you'd call me Cassandra, Atu. Do you have to be formal even when we're dancing together?'

He smiled. 'I call you Miss Cassandra for the same reason the Captain calls the owner Mr Dennison—on a ship of this size, with a large crew, some formality is necessary.'

'You and Nick are going into partnership on a schooner, aren't you? Or have you changed your mind about that?'

'That's been our plan for many years. The only thing which could change it is if we married girls who couldn't get on with each other. A man's love for his wife is stronger than friendship. But I don't think now that's likely to be a problem for us,' added Atu.

Because you both love the same woman and she loves Nick, she thought, with a surge of compassion for him. If only she had realised that, she would never have accused him of failing to understand the pain of a love which wasn't returned.

She wondered if Atu could live with the knowledge that, while he lay in his berth at night, not far away Nick and Eleni might be making love.

The music ended, and he withdrew his arm from her waist and gave a slight bow.

'May I get you a drink, Cassandra?'

As his black-lashed dark eyes smiled down at her, she thought how attractive he was and wondered why he wasn't the one for whom Eleni had fallen.

'Thank you. A long cold one, please.'

As she walked with him to the bar, she thought how perfect it would have been if Nick had fallen in love with her and Eleni had loved Atu. She had a brief golden vision of the four of them sailing the Pacific on a graceful three-master, their children growing up together like brothers and sisters.

But it was only a pipe-dream. Life wasn't like that.

On the way back to Lautoka Harley gave orders for the yacht to call at Beachcomber Island so that anyone who was interested could visit it.

Cassandra was among those who went ashore there. Although she preferred the undeveloped Yasawas, she thought Beachcomber a fun place.

Joanne had not gone ashore. It was plain that she wanted to spend every moment of his free time with Hugh. Those around them made a point of not intruding on them. Some people were expecting them to announce their engagement. Cassandra thought this unlikely. Her guess was that they would test their feelings for each other by separating for a period.

She wanted to talk to her sister about her own imminent departure, but Rosalind had become elusive. At times she was nowhere to be found. More than once when Harley was on deck but Rosalind wasn't, Cassandra went to her own cabin and telephoned the owner's suite in the hope of having a private talk. When there was no reply to several such calls, and it didn't seem likely that Ros had been in the shower, Cassandra began to wonder if her sister was somewhere with Terry. Surely she wouldn't be fool enough to go to his cabin? If Harley found out, he would be justifiably furious.

Terry would probably lose his job and Ros would find herself looking for a new protector. An out-of-work radio officer wouldn't be able to keep her in the style to which she had accustomed herself. Whatever was between them—and Cassandra was baffled by what Ros could see in Terry—would swiftly evaporate in the less rarefied atmosphere of the everyday world.

On the last day of the year, *Ocean Wanderer* was once again berthed at Lautoka where most of the passengers spent the morning ashore buying the components for fancy dress costumes to wear at the New Year's Eve party.

All day Mrs Shane and Eleni were kept busy helping people whose outfits needed some stitching or glueing or painting. Cassandra was borrowing a Minnie Mouse outfit left on board after a previous costume party and kept in Mrs Shane's stores. It consisted of a white blouse and short black skating skirt, a long black velvet tail and a stretchy black cap with the cartoon mouse's large ears. To complete the effect she was going to apply white-face make-up and wear a clown's red bobble nose and a set of untrimmed false eyelashes.

Eleni came to her cabin to stick these in place for her. They had been together most of the day and the Fijian girl had been cheerful and talkative. But now it was obvious that something had happened to upset her. She fixed the spiky black lashes close to Cassandra's own lashes in preoccupied silence.

When the younger girl looked in the mirror at her reflection, and said laughingly, 'Perhaps I should go as Miss Piggy,' Eleni's wan smile was a shadow of her normal one.

'Eleni, something's the matter. What's wrong? Is it Atu again?' Cassandra asked sympathetically. She couldn't imagine what else could have upset her.

For a moment it seemed the other girl was going to deny that anything was troubling her. Then, after some hesitation, she nodded and said, in a depressed tone, 'I don't think Nick's plan is going to work out.'

'What do you mean?' asked Cassandra, puzzled.

Could it be that Eleni had guessed how Atu felt about her and was worried that the two men's long friendship would change to enmity if Nick discovered it?

CHAPTER SEVEN

'NICK was certain Atu would relent if we were together,' said Eleni. 'But I've been on board for a week and each day he's colder towards me. I'm afraid he may not care for me any more.'

Under their double fringe of lashes, Cassandra's eyes widened incredulously as she took in the implications of Eleni's statement.

'You mean it's Atu you want to marry?'

'But of course it's Atu. Who else could it be?'

'I thought it was Nick!'

Eleni looked baffled. 'Nick? What ever gave you that strange idea?'

'You did . . . he did. The evening you came on board I couldn't help overhearing what you said to each other on the quay. It sounded as if it were Nick your parents disapproved of as a husband for you.'

'But Nick and I are like brother and sister. He was the first person to guess how I felt about Atu . . . and how he felt about me.'

'And still does! I'm quite sure of that,' Cassandra told her, with conviction. 'If you could have seen him watching you during the *meke* you'd have no doubts at all, Eleni. I did see him, and it worried me. I felt for them both to be in love with you must create tremendous difficulties, especially with this partnership they're planning.'

'But if he does love me, why is he always so hostile? I'm making no headway at all,' Eleni wailed despairingly. 'He used to have the idea that he wasn't good enough for me because his father was a greaser and he's only a steward; and those were two of the reasons my parents disapproved,' she added. 'But surely I've proved beyond doubt that they aren't important to me? Nick is in favour of our marriage. If he hadn't been, he wouldn't have arranged for me to replace the stewardess who was taken ill.'

'I'm sure, if you stick it out, Atu will admit he loves you and wants to marry you,' said Cassandra.

Although she tried not to show it, her own spirits had been soaring since the discovery of her misunderstanding of the real relationship between Nick and Eleni. Now she was filled with fresh hope that, if she were to follow the advice she had given the other girl and accepted Nick's offer to fix an *au pair* position in Sydney for her, there might yet be a happy future for her.

Then, like a douche of cold water, came the memory of how, to save face, she had told him she was still in love with someone in England.

How could she retract that misleading white lie?

Later, going on deck with the end of her tail in her hand and her face a mask of white make-up with a wide Minnie Mouse mouth lipsticked over her own, she thought with regret of some of the flattering and alluring costumes she could have devised if only Eleni's revelation had come a day sooner.

That she was awarded one of the prizes which the ever-bountiful Harley handed out during the evening was small consolation for seeing in the New Year with a ping-pong ball taped to her nose.

And when, after *Auld Lang Syne*, many people hugged and kissed her as they wished her a happy New Year, Nick confined himself to shaking hands.

Ten days later he asked her if she would like to be on the bridge when the yacht entered Sydney's famous harbour.

Cassandra accepted the invitation eagerly, but she

didn't delude herself that it had any special significance. Throughout the voyage from Fiji he had never been more than ordinarily friendly; and she had failed to think of any way she could make plain that there wasn't and never had been a man in England who had held her heart, even briefly.

Eleni, too, was still in a state of suspense. She couldn't bring herself to force Atu's hand by telling him she loved him. She felt that her presence on *Ocean Wanderer* spoke for itself. The rest was up to him.

There were moments, when they were talking, when Cassandra was tempted to confide how she felt about Nick. But she couldn't quite trust Eleni not to pass on her secret, if only by a broad and well-intentioned hint, and for that reason she said nothing to her.

Cassandra's first impression of Sydney was of pleasant residential suburbs built around dozens of inlets, many of them lined with cruisers and sailing boats. There were many questions she would have liked to ask, but, feeling herself privileged to be the only passenger other than Harley on the bridge, she did her best to efface herself.

The owner didn't share her scruples, but Nick didn't seem to mind his employer's barrage of questions, mostly concerning present-day real estate values rather than the harbour's history.

'So that's the famous Opera House, eh?' said Harley, when the clustered white 'sails' of the city's contribution to world-famous architecture came into view ahead of them.

'That's it. Estimated cost, seven million dollars. Final cost, twenty years later, one hundred and two million,' said Nick. He glanced in Cassandra's direction and she caught the flicker of a wink.

The message that he felt she would share his amusement at Harley's dollars-and-cents attitude to life warmed her. But she knew it was clutching at a straw to read anything of importance into that brief smiling glance.

Merely to stand behind him as he directed the ship's movements with the quiet efficiency of long experience, at the same time making himself pleasant to the owner, made her realise her own inadequacies in comparison with his abilities.

Close to the Opera House was the landmark it had usurped, the great half-moon metal structure which linked the sides of the harbour, carrying a ceaseless shuttle of cars between the crowded highrise blocks of downtown Sydney, to port, and the smaller group of office towers round the end of the bridge on the starboard side.

Here the waterway was busy with ferries, tugs, freighters and tour boats, and the incoming yacht moved more slowly among the criss-cossing harbour traffic. As she glided beneath the bridge, Cassandra noticed a giant clown's face above the entrance to an amusement park on the north bank and a building marked Pier One on the south bank. It appeared to be an old warehouse converted into a complex of shops and cafés. She saw people focusing their cameras on *Ocean Wanderer* as the yacht manoeuvred into position before edging gently alongside a wharf out of sight of the onlookers.

The Customs and Immigration formalities were more stringent in Sydney than they had been in Fiji, and it was some time before anyone could go ashore.

The delay made Rosalind furious. She was impatient to sample the city's shops. She and Harley were going to a party ashore that evening and she wanted to buy a dress for it and spend several hours in a beauty salon.

When it was permitted, Cassandra went ashore with Eleni, who took her to see an historic part of Sydney known as The Rocks, which was only a short walk away from the yacht's berth.

They returned to the ship to be told the Captain wanted to see Cassandra without delay. Remembering the last time she had been summoned to his cabin, she wondered what was in store for her now.

Nick was seated at his desk, wearing civilian clothes, when she entered his day cabin.

He rose to his feet, but he didn't invite her to sit down.

'Ah, Cassandra—back just in time. I'm going to the airport shortly. I've had to change my plans,' he told her. 'Tomorrow I had intended to take you to meet my family. But when I rang up to arrange it, I learned that my mother's father, who lives in Melbourne, hasn't been feeling too good. I'm going to fly there straight away. I'll be back by tomorrow evening and we'll go to Hunters Hill on Sunday. Okay?'

'Of course, but please don't come back tomorrow on my account. Why not spend the whole weekend with your grandfather?'

'It depends how I find him. His housekeeper may be exaggerating—she's inclined to fuss. I shall know when I get there whether I need to stay longer. For the time being, keep Sunday free, will you?'

She nodded. 'I'm sorry you've come home to hear rather worrying news.'

'Thank you.'

For a moment she thought he was going to say something else, but either she was mistaken or he changed his mind. His nod indicated that the conversation was over and he had things to do in the time left before his departure.

That evening, as she had on Cassandra's first night aboard, Rosalind came to her sister's cabin to show her the dress she was wearing for the party. It was an Italian import from one of the expensive boutiques at Double Bay; a clinging sheath of palest grey chiffon, exquisitely beaded, which set off her rich chestnut hair.

With it she was wearing the most beautiful jewel Cassandra had ever seen; a large free-form piece of opal like a chunk of crystallised rainbow.

'Ros! What a wonderful opal,' Cassandra exclaimed, leaning closer to admire it.

'Harley bought it for me this afternoon.'

As she chattered on about the other jewels they had been shown before Harley had picked out the one she was wearing, it seemed to Cassandra there was something strange about her manner. It had been a shock to discover that Rosalind often took sleeping pills. Now, with a pang of disquiet, she wondered if her sister also used drugs to pep her up for occasions such as tonight's party.

With a sudden switch of subject, Rosalind said, 'I hear Nick has gone off to Melbourne. So when is he going to fix up this mother's help job for you?'

'On Sunday, probably.'

'I can't imagine anything I should like less than being a domestic dogsbody, but I expect it will suit you quite well. Playing elder sister to a pack of Aussie kids is more your scene than being the chaste younger sister of a scarlet woman, isn't it?' Ros said sarcastically. 'Don't pretend that's not how you think of me—I know it is. I saw it in your face just now. You looked at my dress and at this——' She touched the fiery opal. 'You knew Harley must have spent a lot of money on me today and it made you cringe. Didn't it?'

'It made me wish Harley loved you and you cared for him,' Cassandra answered, in a low tone.

'Well, he doesn't, and nor do I—and a fat lot of good your crush on Nick Carroll will do you,' added Rosalind, in a hard voice. 'I know you fancy him, so it's no use pretending you don't. But take some advice: don't make the mistake of thinking that because he's suggested this job he's interested in you.' She glanced at the clock. 'I'll have to go—the limousine will be waiting. What are you going to do with yourself tomorrow?'

'Eleni is taking me sightseeing. She knows Sydney. She's lived here.'

'It's typical of you to make friends with a stewardess instead of the people who would have been useful contacts,' said Rosalind critically. Then she shrugged. 'Still, it's your life. We all have to do our own thing.' Unexpectedly, her blue eyes softened. 'I'm sorry it hasn't worked out, Cass. We're not on the same wavelength, are we?'

Even more surprisingly, she darted across the cabin and gave Cassandra a kiss, or rather the fleeting pressure of cheek on cheek which passed for a kiss among women who didn't want to smudge their make-up.

Considering that, minutes earlier, her manner had bordered on hostility, the affectionate gesture before she hurried away left the younger girl puzzled and worried by her sister's abrupt change of mood.

The next morning, Eleni took her to Paddington Market, where they browsed among open-air stalls selling avant-garde clothes designed by art students, jewellery ranging from plastic to gold, leather sandals and belts, hand-painted tee-shirts and a motley assortment of 'antiques' and unashamed junk.

The two girls explored the steep streets of colourful houses until it was time for lunch. Then they went to a health food bar near the market and bought turkey and bean sprout salads wrapped in unleavened bread which they ate sitting on a low wall, watching a street conjuror.

In the afternoon they went to the Art Gallery of New South Wales, an imposing Grecian-style building on the edge of a large open space of grass and tall trees called the Domain.

'What's that huge thing over there, I wonder?' said Cassandra, as they paused between the tall columns of the Gallery's portico after looking at paintings for an hour or more.

The structure she meant looked like the top of an immense circus tent.

'That's where they'll be having the Opera-in-the-Park later this mouth,' Eleni told her. 'If you're not tired, I thought we'd stroll through the Botanic Gardens which will lead us down to the Opera House for you to have a closer look at it.'

It was a very hot day, and when they returned to the yacht both girls were looking forward to a shower and a rest.

'It's been a super day, Eleni. I've enjoyed every minute,' Cassandra said gratefully, before they separated.

Before Eleni could reply, Atu appeared. 'Mr Dennison would like to see you,' he told Cassandra. 'You'll find him in his suite.'

'Thanks, Atu. I'll go right away.' As she walked off she heard him speaking to the other girl in their language. It seemed to her that his tone sounded friendlier than usual.

Harley had a drink in his hand when, after knocking, she entered his private sitting-room. He was alone. Perhaps Ros was in the bedroom.

The air-conditioned coolness was a welcome relief from the humid heat of a summer day in Sydney.

'You look hot,' he said.

She nodded. 'We've walked a long way. Did you enjoy your golf?'

She knew he had spent the whole day on the links. But he had been back on board long enough to have showered and changed.

Harley nodded. 'Sit down, Cassandra.' He indicated an armchair.

The gravity of his expression and the fact that he didn't mention his performance on the links sent a prickle of apprehension through her.

'I'm afraid I have very bad news for you,' he said quietly, when she was seated.

She felt the blood drain from her face . . . her brain . . . her heart. Time stopped. The world ceased to spin. Everything came to a standstill. She seemed to be poised on the brink of a dreadful dark void.

'Dear God . . . not Nick,' she whispered.

'I spoke to Nick half an hour ago. He's getting a lift on a private plane tomorrow morning. He'll be back by around ten o'clock.'

The relief was so overwhelming that it was a moment or two before she realised that something else bad had happened.

Seeing the question dawning in her eyes, Harley said, 'Rosie has left me. She's run off with that bastard Anson. They've gone to the Gold Coast.'

'The Gold Coast?' she echoed, mystified.

'It's the strip of the Queensland coast from the border up past Surfers Paradise. It's where people go to retire, or to play in the sun. I'm told it's a lot like Miami. There's a lot of money up there,' said Harley. He emptied his glass and moved towards the drinks cupboard. 'Can I fix you something?'

Cassandra shook her head. 'No, thanks.' The aftermath of her terror that Nick had been killed was still clouding her mind, making it difficult to think straight.

'Terry has no money,' she said. 'What will they live on?'

'They can raise at least a month's rent on the opal I gave her yesterday,' was his bitter retort.

She had forgotten the opal . . . the costly dress. Now she remembered the strangeness of her sister's behaviour the previous evening. Ros had known they wouldn't be seeing each other again; she had been saying goodbye. But this was no impulsive elopement of lovers who, through force of circumstances, had no other recourse but to run away together. She and Terry had concocted a cold-blooded scheme to milk Harley of every dollar they could wring out of him.

Her sister's callous abuse of the American's generosity made Cassandra stifle a groan.

'Harley ... how could she?' she said, in a horrified whisper.

'Easily, I guess.' He splashed some liquor into his glass and another. 'Have a drink, kid. You've had a shock. Two shocks,' he added, handing the other glass to her.

'When did you find out?'

'There was a note waiting for me when I got back from golf. You can read it if you like.' He crossed to the desk and picked up a single sheet of writing paper which he brought to where she was sitting. When she hesitated to take it, he said, 'Go ahead. If you don't know it already, that letter ought to confirm that your sister is no great loss—to either of us.'

There had been a time when letters written in Rosalind's untidy scrawl had been a lifeline to Cassandra. Now, reluctantly, she read the few unfeeling lines with which Ros had ended her liaison with Harley.

'I can't say it would have surprised me if she'd gone off with somebody richer,' he said. 'The surprise is her picking a guy like Anson. Is he all that attractive to women? I wouldn't have said so.'

'I wouldn't either. I don't know how she could do this. I—I don't know what to say.' She handed back the note.

Harley shrugged. 'It's not your fault, honey. Don't you worry, I'll see you're okay. If this job Nick is trying to arrange doesn't work out, I'll make sure you get back to England. You needn't fret about that.'

'I'm surprised you didn't tell Mrs Shane to pack my things and have me thrown off the ship the moment I came back on board,' Cassandra said bleakly. 'It's what most men would have done in the circumstances.

'If I'd done that, I could have found myself without a captain or a crew,' he answered, with somewhat forced humour. 'You've made a lot of friends since you joined us. With the exception of Anson, none of the officers liked Rosie—I was aware of that. But they like you.'

He raised his drink to his lips, reminding her of the untouched glass she was holding. She took a small sip. It was neat Scotch poured over ice. Harley drank only the best. The whisky had a smooth taste. It didn't burn her palate, but a few moments later she felt a glow spreading inside her. It didn't make her feel better.

The trauma she had experienced at the very beginning of the trip was nothing compared with her present state of mind. With painful clarity, she could visualise the disgust with which Nick would receive the news when he returned tomorrow morning.

How could he want to introduce the sister of someone like Rosalind to his relations? He couldn't. The best thing she could do for him would be to let him off the hook. She wasn't Harley's responsibility, nor was she Nick's. The time had come to stand on her own feet. Somehow she had to get herself and her luggage off *Ocean Wonderer* and lose herself. It shouldn't be hard to do in a city of three million people.'

With neither air-conditioners nor fans, the top floor rooms in old Mrs Murray's delapidated house were like ovens at the end of a boiling mid-January day.

Darlinghurst Road, which Cassandra had to pass through whenever she wanted to catch a bus or a train, was sordid enough by day. What it was like by night she couldn't imagine and didn't intend to find out. But her attic room was very cheap, and if Harley or Nick had made some attempt to find her, after receiving the notes she had left them, the last place they would have looked would be in what Sydneysiders called The Cross.

Altogether she had left four notes on *Ocean*

Wanderer, to be found after she had gone. The others had been to Mrs Shane and Eleni. Shaney had been spending that weekend in her own house. It had been by pretending that she'd been invited to stay with her that Cassandra had been able to get off the ship, with her suitcase, without the seaman on gangway duty suspecting she was leaving for good.

The short letter to Nick had been the most difficult to write. Since then she had spent many hours wondering about his reaction to it when he returned from Melbourne the following morning.

At heart she was rather sorry there was no way he could find her. But her head told her it was wishful thinking to visualise him distraught with worry. If Nick had had any feelings warmer than friendship for her, he would have made them apparent on the voyage from Fiji to Sydney. Instead he had actually avoided opportunities to dance with her at Christmas and New Year and, since then, had been no more than ordinarily pleasant to her.

For several days after her precipitate flight from an impossible situation, Cassandra stayed in her room except when it was necessary to go out for food and exercise.

After a while being cooped up became intolerable. Being afraid that in the city centre she might meet someone from the yacht, she took to going further afield to places such as Parramatta, now an outer suburb of Sydney but originally a separate settlement and one of Australia's most historic localities.

Gradually the shock of Rosalind's defection began to lessen, but, as with all major shocks, it had sapped her normal initiative and left her without the drive to organise her next move.

Every day she scanned the jobs advertised in the *Sydney Morning Herald*, but when she telephoned the number of a motel in need of a maid the vacancy had already been filled, as had a job as a waitress which she applied for.

The *Herald*'s editorial pages were giving considerable coverage to the forthcoming Saturday night performance of Opera in the Park when Australia's world-famous soprano, Dame Joan Sutherland, was going to sing the leading role in *Lucia di Lammermoor*. A hundred thousand Sydneysiders were expected to crowd the Domain, sitting on rugs and cushions, and Cassandra decided to join them.

In such a huge crowd there was little risk of her running into anyone she knew—if indeed *Ocean Wanderer* was still in port. The only way she could be certain of that was by going to the wharf to look, or by ringing the Berthing Master's office. However, she was inclined to think the yacht had probably left Sydney by this time.

The centre of the Domain, from the canopied stage to the lighting towers and beyond them, was a packed mass of people when she arrived at the park. It seemed as if the whole of Sydney had turned out to see their home-grown star soprano who, before Cassandra was born, had made operatic history at London's Covent Garden in the rôle she was singing tonight.

The weather had changed. It was a cool, breezy evening and Dame Joan was wearing a white shawl over her evening dress when her appearance was greeted by a rapturous ovation from the crowd. But as she began to sing her first aria, and the legendary voice, said to be finer now than when she was first acclaimed as one of opera's immortals, filled the park with its glorious sound, a deep hush fell over her listeners.

Cassandra would have been touched by the music in any circumstances. With her own new knowledge of heartbreak, she found it unbearably moving. Unable to hold back her tears, she wiped them away with her hand, knowing no one would notice. They were all intent on the stage and the white-shawled figure, too far away to be seen clearly, whose singing held them enthralled.

When the interval came, Cassandra put on the sweater she had had draped round her shoulders. Most of the people nearby had brought snacks and drinks. For those who hadn't brought picnics there were food stalls with long line-ups round them. She had brought an apple and some biscuits. To stretch her legs after sitting cross-legged for a long time, she ate the apple standing up.

She had taken her second bite when she had the feeling of being watched, and looking around, she saw a boy of about fifteen standing a few feet away. When she looked at him, he smiled and came closer.

'You an Aussie or a tourist?' he asked her.

'I'm a tourist.' Could he be older than he looked?

'Where're you from?'

'England.' Certain he was a schoolboy, she added, 'How about you?'

'I live here.' He was wearing jeans and a navy blue sweater. Hitching up the front of the sweater, he exposed his shirt. A piece of paper showed above the top of the pocket. 'I've got a message for you.'

She stiffened. How could this unknown youth have a message for her?

'I think you must be mistaking me for someone else,' she said.

He handed an envelope to her. 'You are Cassandra Vernon, aren't you?'

'What makes you think that?'

'I've seen a photograph of you ... and Nick described you. He's my uncle. He's been going scatty about you. You'd better read the message.'

'Hold this.' Cassandra gave him the apple, then, her fingers shaking, she ripped the envelope open and withdrew the paper inside. The message was short. In two succinct sentences it changed the world for her.

I love you. I must see you. Nick.

She managed to croak, 'Where is your uncle?'

'He's searching for you over there.' The boy indicated the far side of the Domain. 'There are fifty of us altogether. When Eleni said she felt sure you'd be here tonight, Uncle Nick organised a search party. He said even with this huge crowd, in three hours we ought to spot you. If we didn't, he was going to have your photograph published in the newspaper. But he didn't want to do that in case it got you into trouble with the immigration people—for working without a permit,' he added explanatorily. 'The search has been going on ever since you went missing.'

'How are you going to call it off, now that you've found me?' she queried.

'I'll show you.'

Having handed back the apple, from the pocket of his jeans he produced something long and thin wrapped in a twist of paper and a box of matches. The paper contained several sparklers. The boy lit one and began to whirl it in circles.

'As soon as one of the others sees this, they'll know you've been found and they'll light their sparkler to pass the message right round the Domain.'

Sure enough, within a few moments a sparkling spiral of light appeared far across the park, followed by another and another.

'Now I have to take you to the rendezvous point,' said the boy.

Handing the still fizzing sparkler to one of the several children who had gathered round to watch it, he beckoned Cassandra to follow him.

'The others will stay where they are and watch the rest of the opera. I have to take you to the rendezvous and stay with you till Uncle Nick shows up,' he explained, as they walked under the trees to the roadway in front of the Art Gallery.

'Where is the rendezvous point?'

'The steps over there.' He pointed towards the columned portico where she and Eleni had stood ... it seemed a lifetime ago.

They had hardly arrived at the steps before he said, 'Here comes my uncle,' and Cassandra turned to see a tall figure emerge from the shadows of the trees and break into a run.

'See you later.' The boy melted away and left her standing alone as Nick came charging across the road.

I love you.

She had his note in her hand and he wouldn't have written those words unless, miraculously, he meant them.

She began to run towards him. Moments later she was in his arms for the first time since the earth tremor; laughing and crying, and hugging him almost as tightly as he was hugging her.

'Thank God you're safe!' His voice was so ragged it didn't sound like his at all.

When she looked up into his face she could see that, like her, he had lost weight. It showed in the sharper outlines of the bones of his cheeks and jaw. He looked haggard with worry and tiredness, and she saw with wonder and pain the glitter of tears in his eyes.

'I love you, too,' she whispered. 'Oh, Nick, I love you so much!'

There was no more to say. Or not yet. Not until several lingering kisses had confirmed, much better than words, that being in each other's arms was, for them both, the best, the only place to be.

Then they sat on the Gallery steps while Cassandra explained where she had been and Nick told her of his frantic efforts to find her.

They might have sat there all night if another tumultuous ovation from the great crowd in the park hadn't made him say, with a smile, 'You're going to have to tell your grandchildren that, although you were here tonight, you missed the high point of the opera—the Mad Scene.'

They didn't miss the end of the performance, because the Mad Scene was followed by the tenor's chance to outshine the dramatic climax of the soprano's part. When the last act was over, they were in the Domain to see the audience rise from the grass, cheering and clapping in a storm of applause which must have been heard on the other side of the harbour.

'And now, my darling,' said Nick, when La Stupenda had taken her final call, 'the others are going to celebrate our engagement, but you and I are going to have a private party.'

Cassandra woke up the next morning in a brass four-poster curtained with folds of white muslin tied back with pale blue silk ribbons.

Sunlight enhanced the sheen of a waxed and polished board floor covered, in the centre of the bedroom, by a blue and white needlework carpet. The chests of drawers, chairs and tables were all lovingly cared for antiques, and the room had a brick-backed fireplace filled with pots of ferns inside a burnished brass fender.

For a while she lay still, enjoying her charming surroundings and remembering the events of last night.

Nick had walked her back to Kings Cross to collect her belongings. Then a cruising taxi had brought them across the harbour to this lovely old Hunters Hill house owned by his uncle, Robert Carroll, and his wife Mary.

They had welcomed her warmly, as if there were nothing extraordinary about her arrival. Robert had opened champagne, then Mary had produced a light after-theatre supper. When they had talked for an hour or so, Nick had swept Cassandra upstairs to the room prepared for her and shown considerable reluctance at leaving her to sleep alone.

She would have been happy for him to stay. But eventually he had torn himself out of her arms and muttered a husky good night. She thought it was largely consideration for his relatives' scruples which had made him go to his own room. Certainly Cassandra herself would not have objected if his tender caresses had led to their rightful conclusion.

She was wondering how long it would be before they could share a bed and spend the whole night together, when there was a knock at the door.

'Come in.'

Expecting it to be Mary Carroll, she was pleased to find it was Nick. She sat up, bright-eyed and refreshed after the best night's rest she had had in a long time.

'Good morning. How did you sleep?'

He had obviously just had a shower. His dark hair was still wet. He was wearing a white terry bathrobe.

'On Cloud Ninety,' she told him, laughing.

Nick sat down on the bed. 'Me, too. I had a lot of sleepless nights to make up. I went out like a light as soon as I hit the mattress.' He drew her into his arms and kissed her forehead, the tip of her nose and her mouth.

'I like you like this ... tousled and cuddly,' he murmured, a little while later.

She nestled against him, aware that one ruffled strap had slipped off the curve of her shoulder and the front of her nightie was gaping, exposing the tops of her breasts. Once, she would have hurriedly covered herself. Now she wouldn't have minded if he had pushed it down further. She wanted him to touch her, and to touch him. Her hand, resting on his chest, moved from the rough white towelling to the smooth bronzed skin in the vee between the lapels. It gave her a deep thrilling pleasure to stroke her fingertips lightly on his warm flesh; and it seemed to please him as well.

Nick put her away from him. His voice rather ragged,

he said, 'I came to suggest we had breakfast together on the balcony, but if we carry on like this——' He left the sentence in the air.

Her hands at the back of his neck, Cassandra gave him an innocent look. Caressing him behind the ears, she asked, 'What will happen?'

'More than my aunt would like,' he told her dryly. 'And as we're going to be married almost immediately, I think we can wait a little longer, don't you?'

She considered the question. 'I can ... if you can,' she teased him.

Nick grinned. 'I'd find it easier if you were on the other side of a table and a good deal more covered up! The way you look at the moment is enough to tempt a saint. I'm going down to fix the breakfast.'

By the time he came back with a tray, Cassandra had discovered that the balcony outside her room overlooked a small wooded creek, an inlet off a larger waterway.

Nick reappeared and asked her to spread a cloth on the white wooden table outside her room. Then they unloaded the tray.

'Nick, what about Eleni and Atu?' she asked, as he drew out a chair for her. 'Is he still refusing to admit he loves her?'

'No, that was one good result of your going into hiding. It seemed to make Atu realise how he would feel if she took it into her head to follow your bad example.'

'What else could I do? When Harley announced that Ros had left him, I felt so ashamed ... for us both.'

'Harley told me she took him for several thousand dollars the day before she walked out on him,' said Nick. 'But you're not your sister's keeper and you have no need to feel guilty about her behaviour. It was clear to us all from the outset that the two of you were chalk and cheese. Although I have to admit that the first time I saw you, with a lot of paint on your face and a dress which wasn't your style, I did wonder if you were two of a kind. I soon changed my mind about that,' he added.

'You didn't behave as if you had. Did Eleni tell you I thought you had arranged for her to join the cabin crew because you were in love with her?'

'Yes, she did—but she couldn't give me any clue to your feelings about me. I thought as she had taken you into her confidence, you would have reciprocated. The fact that you hadn't seemed to confirm you were still hankering after the guy in England.'

'Who was an invention,' she admitted. 'There was never anyone in England. I made him up because I was terrified you'd guessed how I felt about you. But if I convinced you he did exist, or had existed, when did you stop believing in him?'

'Not until I came back from Melbourne to the news that you'd disappeared. Harley told me that, when he told you something bad had happened, you said something like, *Oh, God—not Nick*, and looked as if you were going to faint. "That kid's in love with you, Nick. No doubt about it," he said to me. And I began to believe that perhaps you were—in spite of a lot of evidence to the contrary.'

'What evidence?' she asked, curious to hear his view of their relationship.

They had finished their grapefruit, and Nick lifted a silver-plated cover from a large dish of grilled bacon, liver, mushrooms and tomatoes. As he transferred the food to their plates, putting all the choicest things on hers, she noticed, he said, 'Mainly your reaction to being kissed. But there were other things. When I tried to warm your hands at the crater, you snatched them away as if you couldn't bear me to touch you.'

'It wasn't five minutes since I'd looked round to find you glaring as if you couldn't stand the sight of me. And that was the time when I thought you and Joanne were involved, or going to be involved.'

'If I was glaring, it was at Hugh, not at you, my sweet goose,' Nick told her. 'As for Joanne, I remember thinking on the drive up to the crater that it would do Hugh good to spend some time in her bed if she was agreeable.'

'Do you think they did sleep together before she went back to California?' she asked. 'Do you think anything will come of it?'

'The answer to both those questions is—I don't know. But it's likely that pretty soon Hugh's going to be in a better position to ask her to marry him. I'm going to ask Harley to release me from my contract, which I think he will, and I'll recommend Hugh as my successor. If, after a separation, Hugh and Joanne think they've got a future together, he can make it a condition of his contract that he has his wife on board with him.'

'I'm sure she'd love that and make a marvellous Captain's wife. Poor Harley! Losing you and Atu and probably Mrs Shane as well, because I don't think she'll stay on *Ocean Wanderer* without you. That reminds me, when Atu was telling me the legend of *tagimoucia*, he said some of your relations had a room full of your mother's flower paintings. Are they in this house?'

Nick nodded. 'After breakfast I'll show you.' He passed her the toast rack. 'Harley was quite upset that you'd enclosed the pendant he gave you at Christmas with the note you left for him.'

'I hated having to accept it in the first place. I couldn't possibly have kept it after what happened.'

The thought of her sister was the one cloud on her horizon. Reading her thoughts, Nick reached for her hand.

'Don't worry about her. She's a very tough cookie. She'll get by, after her fashion.'

'I suppose so. But I can't help feeling sorry she'll never have this kind of happiness,' she answered, as he pressed a kiss on each of her knuckles.

'Or want it,' said Nick. 'Being a charter skipper's wife wouldn't suit your sister at all. We shan't be well off, Cassandra. Atu and I believe we can make a comfortable living, but the charter business is very dependent on the world economic situation. There may be times when we all have to tighten our belts.'

'We shall be rich in all the important things,' she said confidently. 'Nick, when did you know you loved me?'

'Do you remember the afternoon you drove to Hana with Hugh and I told you to spend less time with him?'

'How could I forget it? I thought you were going to kiss me again, but you didn't.'

'I was going to when it suddenly hit me that the reason I thought Hugh was in danger of losing his heart to you was because I'd already lost mine. When you told me he was the only person on board you felt comfortable with, I was as jealous as hell,' Nick admitted.

'How unexpected life is,' she murmured. 'A year ago, Australia wasn't even on the list of places I wanted to visit. As for marrying an Australian . . .'

He turned her into his arms. 'We must organise that right away. I've waited a long time to find you, my lovely girl.' He bent his tall head to hers.

Eleni and Atu were married twice, and Nick was groomsman at both weddings. For the Methodist church service, Eleni wore a white lace dress and her black hair was starred with white flowers.

But at the Fijian ceremony which took place later the same day, she looked even more beautiful, barefoot and wearing a skirt of creamy *tapa* cloth patterned with designs in black and tan. A garland of curly bark shavings and wild flowers was her only adornment as she walked with slow dignity to the bride's mat, followed by the women of her family and the uncle who was giving her away.

Atu and Nick were also wearing skirts of *tapa* and

garlands. Most men of European origin would have looked and felt ill at ease in the Fijian costume, but with Nick's fine physique and deep tan he looked as splendid as Atu. Cassandra felt a thrill of pride at the sight of her husband supporting his closest friend as Atu had supported him at his wedding in Sydney a week earlier.

She was wearing the simple short dress of ivory chiffon in which she herself had been married as she watched and took photographs of Eleni and Atu being joined in the ancient way. When Eleni's father held up the large polished whale's tooth which, in times gone by, had been of vital importance in Fijian life, a strange sound known as the *tama* was made by the island-born onlookers. And although she was a modern girl with advanced ideas on a woman's place in society, Eleni looked very happy to be bestowed as a gift to the bridegroom's family.

Hours later, when the feast was over Nick and Cassandra returned to their hotel.

As she hung her dress in the closet of their room, Nick came up behind her and dropped the garland he had been wearing over her head. His fingers brushed against her spine as he unclipped her bra and pushed the straps off her shoulders. A moment later his hands had replaced the lace cups.

Gently fondling her small round breasts, he said, close to her ear, 'For the past two hours I've been thinking how good it would be to be back in an air-conditioned room, re-consummating our marriage. Did the same thought occur to you?'

She nodded, relaxing against him, luxuriating in the first delicious caresses which, at the end of their wedding day, had been her introduction to the pleasures of their private night life.

'I hope Eleni's honeymoon is as blissful as mine,' she murmured.

Nick's strong hands slid possessively down her slim body before he swung her off her feet and carried her across to the bed where last night she had slept in his arms, and this morning had been woken by his kisses.

'Darling!'

All her passionate love for him was in the endearment she whispered as Nick stooped to lay her down and she spread her hands on his shoulders and pulled him down beside her.

When a maid had turned down the bed, she had left on each pillow a flower; a freshly-plucked frangipani. Propped on one elbow, his burning gaze scanning Cassandra's flushed excited face and parted lips, Nick took one of the flowers and stroked it lightly down her body from the base of her throat to her navel.

A faint smile lurked round his mouth as he left the flower there and, with the other, repeated the delicate caress of the fragile white petals against her warm quivering skin.

The subtle tropical fragrance of the frangipani petals, crushed between their bodies in the final moments of ecstatic fusion, lingered in the air as, sharing a pillow, they slept.

Coming Next Month in Harlequin Presents!

847 LION OF DARKNESS Melinda Cross
The New York doctor, who's helped so many cope with blindness in a sighted world, is baffled by his latest case—and a force that threatens the doctor–patient relationship.

848 THE ARROGANT LOVER Flora Kidd
A young widow distrusts the man who tries to come between her and her Scottish inheritance. He made love to her, then left without a word nine years ago. Why should she trust him now?

849 GIVE ME THIS NIGHT Vanessa James
Passion flares between a tour guide and a mystery writer on the Greek island of Paxos. But she's blundered into his life at the worst possible moment —because around him, she senses danger!

850 EXORCISM Penny Jordan
Once she naively assumed he'd marry her if they made love. Now he wants her to help him research his new book in the Caribbean. Why? To exorcise the past?

851 SLEEPING DESIRE Charlotte Lamb
After a year apart, can an estranged wife forget the solicitor's letters and the divorce proceedings? Easily—when the man she loves reawakens her desire.

852 THE DEVIL'S PRICE Carole Mortimer
The day she left him, their love turned to ashes. But a London singer is willing to bargain with the devil to be with her lover again—but not as his wife!

853 SOUTH SEAS AFFAIR Kay Thorpe
Against her better judgment, against all her values, a young woman allows herself to be drawn into a passionate affair with her father's archenemy!

854 SUN LORD'S WOMAN Violet Winspear
Fate, which seemed to have been so kind, deals a cruel blow to a young woman on her wedding night, and her husband's desert kingdom loses its dreamlike appeal.

Here's how to get this special offer from Harlequin!

DECEMBER
TREASURY EDITION
COUPON

As simple as 1...2...3!

1. Each month, save one Treasury Edition coupon from your favorite Romance or Presents novel.
2. In four months you'll have saved four Treasury Edition coupons (<u>only one coupon per month allowed</u>).
3. Then all you have to do is fill out and return the order form provided, along with the four Treasury Edition coupons required and $1.00 for postage and handling.

Mail to: Harlequin Reader Service

RT1-E-2

In the U.S.A.
2504 West Southern Ave.
Tempe, AZ 85282

In Canada
P.O. Box 2800, Postal Station A
5170 Yonge Street
Willowdale, Ont. M2N 6J3

Please send me my FREE copy of the Janet Dailey Treasury Edition. I have enclosed the four Treasury Edition coupons required and $1.00 for postage and handling along with this order form.

(Please Print)

NAME_____

ADDRESS_____

CITY_____

STATE/PROV._____ ZIP/POSTAL CODE_____

SIGNATURE_____

This offer is limited to one order per household.

SUPPLIES LIMITED

This special Janet Dailey offer expires January 1986.

Author **JOCELYN HALEY**, also known by her fans as **SANDRA FIELD** and **JAN MACLEAN**, now presents her eighteenth compelling novel.

With the help of the enigmatic Bryce Sanderson, Kate MacIntyre begins her search for the meaning behind the nightmare that has haunted her since childhood. Together they will unlock the past and forge a future.

Available at your favorite retail outlet in NOVEMBER.

Take 4 best-selling love stories FREE
Plus get a FREE surprise gift!

WORLDWIDE LIBRARY IS YOUR TICKET TO ROMANCE, ADVENTURE AND EXCITEMENT

Experience it all in these big, bold Bestsellers— Yours exclusively from WORLDWIDE LIBRARY WHILE QUANTITIES LAST

To receive these Bestsellers, complete the order form, detach and send together with your check or money order (include 75¢ postage and handling), payable to WORLDWIDE LIBRARY, to:

In the U.S.
WORLDWIDE LIBRARY
Box 52040
Phoenix, AZ
85072-2040

In Canada
WORLDWIDE LIBRARY
P.O. Box 2800, 5170 Yonge Street
Postal Station A, Willowdale, Ontario
M2N 6J3

- -

Quant.	Title	Price
_____	**ANTIGUA KISS,** Anne Weale	$2.95
_____	**WILD CONCERTO,** Anne Mather	$2.95
_____	**STORMSPELL,** Anne Mather	$2.95
_____	**A VIOLATION,** Charlotte Lamb	$3.50
_____	**LEGACY OF PASSION,** Catherine Kay	$3.50
_____	**SECRETS,** Sheila Holland	$3.50
_____	**SWEET MEMORIES,** LaVyrle Spencer	$3.50
_____	**FLORA,** Anne Weale	$3.50
_____	**SUMMER'S AWAKENING,** Anne Weale	$3.50
_____	**FINGER PRINTS,** Barbara Delinsky	$3.50
_____	**DREAMWEAVER,** Felicia Gallant/Rebecca Flanders	$3.50
_____	**EYE OF THE STORM,** Maura Seger	$3.50
_____	**HIDDEN IN THE FLAME,** Anne Mather	$3.50
	YOUR ORDER TOTAL	$_____
	New York and Arizona residents add appropriate sales tax	$_____
	Postage and Handling	$___.75
	I enclose	$_____

NAME _____

ADDRESS _____ APT.# _____

CITY _____

STATE/PROV. _____ ZIP/POSTAL CODE _____
WW2